Katy's Pony Surprise

Katy's Pony Surprise

Victoria Eveleigh

Illustrated by Chris Eveleigh

Orion
Children's Books

First published in Great Britain
under the title *Katy's Exmoor Friends* in 2005
by Tortoise Publishing
This edition first published in 2012
by Orion Children's Books
a division of the Orion Publishing Group Ltd
Orion House
5 Upper St Martin's Lane
London WC2H 9EA
An Hachette UK Company

1 3 5 7 9 10 8 6 4 2

A catalogue record for this book is
available from the British Library.

ISBN 978 1 4440 0553 0

Printed in Great Britain by Clays Ltd, St Ives plc

www.orionbooks.co.uk

For my husband, Chris, with much love and many thanks for helping me in countless ways, including drawing the illustrations for this trilogy.

Exmoor

Contents

1

New Neighbours

As Katy rode her Exmoor pony, Trifle, along the lane from Barton Farm, she felt she was the luckiest girl in the world. Although it was odd to think about Christmas on the first day of the summer holidays, Katy decided she felt the same sort of excitement as on Christmas morning when there was a stocking full of presents at the end of her bed. Also, she thought, holidays are like Christmas stockings because most things are half-expected but there are always some complete surprises tucked in-between. For instance, this summer she knew there'd be horse shows, Pony Club camp, picnics, long rides, lazy days and having fun with her best friend, Alice. But the surprises – well, if she knew what they were going to be, they wouldn't be surprises.

"Next week it's Pony Club camp, Trifle. I'm afraid you'll have to go because poor old Jacko's still lame from that horrid nail he trod on last winter. Anyway, it'll do you good to have a bit of proper schooling. You'll learn how to jump too; that'll be fun!" Katy leaned forward and pretended to ride like a jockey. Trifle felt the shift in her weight and accelerated into a canter. Laughing at the eagerness of her pony, Katy sat up straight again and closed her fingers gently on the reins. Trifle eased back into a steady trot.

They rounded a sharp bend and skidded to a halt. Katy bumped her nose on Trifle's neck, and just managed to save herself from falling off by grabbing a handful of bushy mane.

The lane was blocked by a huge removal lorry. A couple of men in blue overalls, supervised by a dark-haired man wearing a black leather jacket and blue jeans, were using a very noisy electric ramp to unload furniture.

"Oh!" Katy exclaimed. "Wellsworthy Farm must have been sold. That was quick! We can't get past the lorry, so I suppose we'll have to turn back."

"Hi, there!" the man in the leather jacket shouted,

raising his hand in greeting. "Hang on a minute!"

Katy tried her best to hang on a minute; Trifle was dancing on the spot with agitation. The man's eyes were hidden by expensive-looking sunglasses but, as he came closer, Katy could see a smile on his lined, suntanned face. He gave Trifle a hearty pat on the neck, which was more like hitting than patting, and she tried to shy away.

"Nice little Shetland pony you've got there," the man said, nimbly avoiding Trifle's hooves as they tap-danced on the tarmac. "I've just bought this place. Who are you? I'm Dean, by the way."

Katy was just about to speak when Dean gave Trifle another slap and asked, "What's his name?"

Trifle spun round, pushing him to one side.

"Oops! Sorry!" Katy said. "I'm Katy Squires, and I live at Barton Farm, about a mile up that lane. This is my Exmoor pony, Trifle. She's only four, so she gets a bit nervous about new things like removal lorries. And she's a mare – a girl, not a boy."

"Exmoor, Shetland, mare, stallion – they're all the same to me, I'm afraid. Dangerous at both ends and uncomfortable in the middle. Hang about! You're the girl who was on the telly with a pony who saved somebody's life! Is that the pony?" Dean gave Trifle another hit-pat, and she decided she'd had enough.

"Yes, she rescued Granfer – my grandfather. Sorry!

3

Got to go! Nice to meet you!" Katy said quickly, as Trifle set off down the lane, cantering sideways.

"I like the circus trick!" Dean called out. "What d'you do for an encore?"

Katy barely heard him above the noise of Trifle's clattering hooves as she flew round the corner, heading for the safety of home.

Katy's mum was in the kitchen at Barton Farm, talking on the telephone. She broke off from her conversation as Katy appeared. "Boots off! And what are you doing with that bucket?"

"I just need a bucket of warm water from the sink so I can wash Trifle," Katy replied. "She's all sweaty."

Mum sighed. "Go on then, but don't spill any." Her attention returned to the telephone. "Sorry, Melanie. Where was I? Yes, the new kitchen's wonderful, but I don't know how long I'll manage to keep it that way," she said, watching as Katy struggled to squeeze the bucket under the elegant mixer tap of the new sink.

"Oh, are you talking to Alice's mum?" Katy asked.

"Yes, attempting to."

"Can you ask if it's okay for me to go over to Stonyford this afternoon? Alice and I want to get everything sorted for camp."

"Melanie heard you, and she says that's fine. She'll

give you a lesson on Trifle if you get there by two-thirty. We're having salad for lunch as it's such a hot day, so you can have it early if you like."

"Ideal! Thanks!" Katy said, sloshing water onto the floor as she carried the heavy, steaming bucket to the door. "Oops, sorry!" she called over her shoulder.

After she'd washed Trifle, Katy turned her out into the field with Jacko so her coat would dry in the sunshine. She watched while her ponies greeted each other like long-lost friends. Then Trifle wandered away, pawed the ground, circled, crumpled, rolled, sat up for a moment and clambered to her feet again, shaking herself and snorting with satisfaction before settling down to the serious business of eating as much grass as possible.

Even now, Katy found it hard to believe she actually owned the two ponies. She'd bought Trifle as a newly weaned foal from Brendon pony sale, and had kept her in secret at Stonyford for her first winter. During that time, Melanie had taught her to ride on Jacko, a handsome liver chestnut gelding Katy had loved from the start. Granfer had found out about Trifle while he was arranging to buy Jacko for Katy as a present, and on her birthday she'd had the biggest surprise of her life when both Jacko and Trifle had arrived at Barton Farm. Over three years had passed since that day, but she still remembered every detail. She smiled to herself as she watched Jacko and Trifle grazing side by side.

Katy sometimes wondered what her life would be like if Alice hadn't moved to Stonyford with her mum and twin brothers. She probably wouldn't own Trifle, certainly wouldn't own Jacko and she wouldn't have a best friend – not like Alice, anyway. Also, if she really thought about it, Barton Farm would have been sold by now, her family would be miserable and Mum most definitely wouldn't have a brand new kitchen, paid for with the income from Dad's paintings. In fact, Granfer could be . . . Yes, it was scary thinking about what life would be like if the Gardners hadn't moved into Stonyford.

"Lunch time!" Mum called.

"Coming!" Katy replied, and after one last look at the ponies she hurried indoors.

"I thought you said you were just going for a gentle hack this morning. How come Trifle got so sweaty?" Mum asked as she sliced a home-made loaf fresh from the Aga.

The smell of the bread made Katy realise how hungry she was. "I meant to go for a gentle hack, but Trifle had other ideas. It wasn't her fault, though – not really. You see, we met the man who's bought Wellsworthy. He was there with a removal lorry, and he came up to say hello."

"Really? What's he like?"

"Well, Trifle didn't think much of him. He wears those odd sunglasses which look like mirrors, and he obviously doesn't know the first thing about horses – he's one of those people who thinks the right way to greet a horse is to slap it. Oh, and he's called Dean."

Mum looked amused. "Poor Dean! It appears he's managed to fall out with his most important neighbour, an Exmoor pony, before he's even set foot in his new home!"

Trifle looked very surprised and rather grumpy when Katy caught her, tacked her up and set off on another ride after lunch. However, she soon perked up, especially when she realised where they were going. She seemed to love Stonyford almost as much as Katy did.

They took the field and moorland route, avoiding the Wellsworthy lane. Riding through the fields meant going through several gates, but Katy didn't mind because she was trying to teach Trifle how to open them.

It's amazing how quickly she learns new things once she understands what she's supposed to do, Katy thought, as Trifle headed for the correct end of the gate onto the Common, then stood with her head over it and her body close to the post so Katy could undo the latch. "Push it," she said, and Trifle pushed the gate open with her chest, walked through on command, turned in a tight circle and stood still on the other side while Katy did up the latch again. "Good girl!" she said, stroking Trifle's neck. "What a clever pony you are."

They had plenty of time, thanks to an early lunch, so Katy had decided they should walk most of the way to save Trifle's energy for their lesson with Melanie. However, Trifle jigged around so much once they were on the Common that Katy couldn't resist letting her gallop some of the way.

"Yippee! Hurray for the holidays!" Katy shouted as Trifle raced over the heather.

Despite their gallop, the journey seemed to take longer than usual, probably because Katy couldn't wait to see Alice again. They'd remained best friends even though they now went to different schools; Katy went to the local secondary school and Alice went to a boarding school miles away. This made the holidays even more special, and they spent as much time as possible with each other. There was so much Katy wanted to tell Alice, including the news about Wellsworthy.

At last they reached the back entrance to Stonyford, and Trifle announced their arrival with an excited whinny. Katy giggled; it was like sitting on a mini-earthquake when Trifle whinnied.

Alice ran to the gate, opened it and bowed with a flourish. "Behold! Trifle the Wonder Horse!" she announced with extreme grandness. "Are you too famous to grace our humble home now you're a TV celebrity? We'll have to feed you chocolate-coated apples and put champagne in your water buckets."

"She's fizzy enough as it is, thanks," Katy said. "I had a job to stop her on the Common just now."

"Why, hello!" said Alice in mock surprise. "I didn't see you up there!"

"Well, I'd better come down to your level then," Katy replied. She made a clicking sound with her tongue, and Trifle instantly dropped her head to the ground so Katy could slide down her neck. "Tra-lah! That's our latest trick."

"Trifle! Is there no end to your talents?" Alice asked.

The girls laughed. Little did they know they'd soon find out.

2

Pony Club Camp

Camp was one of the highlights of the Pony Club year. On Exmoor, two camps were held in the summer: one for the seniors at the beginning of the holidays and one for the juniors later on. Junior camp wasn't really a camp at all, because the riders and their ponies went home every evening, but at senior camp the horses and ponies were stabled overnight and the riders stayed in tents or caravans.

Katy and Alice had attended junior camp several times, but this would be their first year as seniors. They'd been planning everything for weeks, mostly by text and email, but now it was all becoming real as they packed the things they'd need into Melanie's caravan on the evening before they were due to leave.

"This already feels like home, doesn't it? Our own little house, for five whole nights!" Katy said, stuffing some clothes into one of the neat cupboards above her bed.

Alice sat at the foldaway table by the end window. "Yes, thank goodness Mum said we could take it. Imagine what it would be like fitting all our things into a tent?" She picked up a long list which had been lying on the table. "Right, we'd better check everything's here. This is for each of us, okay? Here goes: two water buckets . . . two feed buckets . . . one tack cleaning bucket and kit . . . two hay nets . . . head collar . . . sweat rug . . . bridle . . . saddle . . . each grooming kit should have a body brush, dandy brush, curry comb, mane comb, hoof pick, two sponges, stable rubber, hoof oil and brush . . ."

The list seemed endless, but at last the final item was checked. Katy plonked herself down on the cushioned seat opposite Alice. "Phew!" she said. "It's a miracle, but I think we've got everything."

"I see we've both bought new buckets and grooming things," Alice said.

Katy laughed. "Yes, I thought it would be *so*

embarrassing to turn up with the old sheep mineral buckets I usually use for water, or the brushes our new sheepdog puppy chewed, so I went to the tack shop last weekend. Everyone going to camp must have had the same idea, because there were hardly any brushes or buckets left and I got the last pair of jods in my size. I'll have to use my old jods as spares, even though they're much too short."

"I thought you'd grown taller since the Easter holidays," said Alice. "We'll both have to ride horses soon."

"Oh, please don't say that!" Katy said. "It's just not fair – when I was younger I longed to be tall like you, but now I'm desperate to stop growing because I want to carry on riding Trifle. There's so much more I want to do with her before I set her free again."

"Set her free?" Alice exclaimed. "That's crazy, after all the work you've done taming her!"

"No it isn't. I've made a promise to her, you see. She's given me so much, and eventually I'm going to give her the greatest gift I can in return, which has to be her freedom. I'm sure if she were given the choice she'd want to be running with the herd on the Common again, having foals of her own." The thought of Trifle with a foal by her side always gave Katy butterflies.

"Trifle's a very lucky pony, to have an owner like you," Alice said.

Katy smiled. "No, I'm the lucky one, to have a pony like Trifle."

Her friends at camp all seemed to think she was lucky as well. As they settled in on the first evening, everyone wanted to meet Trifle. A tame Exmoor pony was a bit of a novelty – even on Exmoor – so a tame *and* famous Exmoor pony was irresistible. They'd seen all the television reports and newspaper articles about her medal for the daring rescue earlier in the year.

"She's so adorable!" said Fiona.

"I love her colour, with those blonde highlights in her mane!" said Sophie.

"And those light bits around her muzzle and eyes," agreed Susan.

Claire hugged Trifle's neck. "I want one!" she declared.

"She can even do tricks, can't she, Katy?" Alice said.

"Well, sort of," Katy replied. "But I hope the only tricks she'll do this week will be to canter on the correct leg and jump when she's asked to."

Her friends laughed, but now that Katy had arrived at camp she realised how small and inexperienced Trifle was compared with the other horses and ponies. Some people her age already had horses which were over fifteen hands high. They looked enormous beside Trifle, who was only twelve-two. Claire had wasted no time in telling everyone about all the prizes her new horse had won with his previous owner.

"Do you think I'm being unfair on Trifle, bringing her here?" Katy asked Alice as they lay in their sleeping bags later that evening, tired and still rather damp after a girls versus boys water fight by the stream.

"What d'you mean?" Alice asked sleepily.

"I'm beginning to think I shouldn't have come this year. Jacko knows all about Pony Club events and jumping and things, but Trifle doesn't. I don't think she's ready for camp yet."

"You worry too much. She'll be fine. Night, night." Almost immediately, Alice started snoring gently.

Katy lay awake for a long time, worrying.

After breakfast the following morning, there was a scramble to see the list of riders and teachers. The classes were numbered from one to six, with the most experienced riders in class one and the least experienced in class six.

"You're with Fiona and me in class four, Katy!" Sophie said, squeezing her way out of the scrum. "Needless to say, Alice and Claire are in class two, but we've got Tony, so they'll be well jealous!" Tony was a volunteer instructor from the King's Troop Royal Horse Artillery, and the girls had already decided he deserved the prize for the best-looking teacher of all time.

Trifle was tense with excitement as Katy groomed her and tacked her up with fumbling fingers. I must be calm, Katy thought, or my nervousness will make her worse.

A bossy-looking instructress marched passed, yelling, "Two minutes! You should be mounted and in line with other members of your class in two minutes!"

Katy quickly dabbed some hoof oil onto each of Trifle's hooves before leading her out of the stable. Most of the others were already mounted and in line, and she felt several eyes on her as she pulled down her stirrups. Trifle pawed the ground impatiently.

"Stand!" Katy said, and put her left foot into the stirrup, ready to mount. Then she sprung with her right foot and lifted herself into the saddle – or she would have done if the saddle hadn't swivelled round to meet her, ending up under Trifle's tummy.

Alarmed by the terrifying dangly object underneath her, Trifle started bucking while Katy held on to her reins and tried to soothe her with gentle words. *Idiot! I'm a complete idiot!* she said to herself, feeling her cheeks glowing bright red with embarrassment. Why on earth didn't I check the girth? I always check the girth before I get on. That's what comes of hurrying too much. She didn't have to look up to know everyone was looking as Trifle plunged in circles around her.

The bossy instructress stormed up and grabbed hold of Trifle. "Stand still, you lunatic!" she commanded. With a couple of deft moves, she undid the girth and removed the saddle. She glared at Katy. "Always check the girth before you mount. Don't they teach you anything at this Pony Club?" With ruthless efficiency, she put the saddle on Trifle's back and heaved up the girth as far as possible. Then she pointed at the neat row of riders facing them. "Look, you're holding everyone up."

Katy's cheeks burned even more as she mounted and rode over to join class four.

Tony smiled at her sympathetically. "Don't worry, we've all done it. You can't learn from your mistakes if you don't make any," he said kindly.

Katy decided she liked Tony a lot.

Trifle tried her best, but Katy could tell she was struggling. She was the smallest pony in the class by far. When the ride was walking, Trifle had to jog to keep up, and when they were trotting, she cantered. Also, it was obvious that the other horses and ponies were much more experienced and well-schooled, especially when they started jumping. Unfortunately the poles were painted bright colours, and Trifle wouldn't even walk over them.

"Perhaps she thinks they're snakes or something," Katy said as Trifle half-reared and leapt away from the poles on the ground in front of her yet again.

"Whatever it is, I don't think this is doing her much good," Tony said. "I'll try leading her."

They tried it with Tony leading her and with Trifle following the other ponies, but nothing seemed to work. Eventually Katy got off and managed to lead her over one pole, which she jumped with a huge leap, as if it were going to bite her. Katy knew they were taking up too much time, so she offered to wait in the centre of the ring while the others did some jumping. Watching them, she couldn't help longing for Jacko. He was really good at jumping. In fact, he was so good at everything that he made riding effortless. It was easy to be a good rider if your pony knew exactly what to do.

At the end of the lesson all the riders dismounted, ran their stirrups up, loosened their girths and walked their horses and ponies back to the stables for a lunch break.

"Katy? Can you hang on a minute?" Tony said.

"Ooh! Aren't you the lucky one?" Sophie teased.

Katy knew she wasn't. She waited for Tony, dreading what he was going to say.

"I think Trifle is a lovely pony, and you ride her very well, Katy."

She waited for the "but".

"But she's still young and rather green, isn't she? I'm worried that we might be teaching her to run before she can walk, so to speak. She's such a willing little pony, and I don't want to frighten her with difficult things before she's learned the basics. Do you think it would be better, for her sake, if she were in class six? I gather they're going to be doing a musical ride, which will be a really good way of making flatwork enjoyable for her."

Katy didn't know what to say. She liked Tony and wanted to stay in his class, but knew that she and Trifle were way out of their depth there. They'd probably end up holding everyone back – the dunces of class four. "Okay. Whatever you think would be best for Trifle," she said, trying to hide her disappointment.

At lunch, Alice and Katy's other friends were sympathetic, but they all agreed that class six would probably be better for Trifle as she'd never jumped before. Katy couldn't help noticing that Tony was talking to the bossy instructress at a table in the far corner, and that she didn't look pleased.

Just when it seems that things can't get much worse, they do, Katy said to herself as she trotted around a dusty arena for the umpteenth time that afternoon, following a reluctant boy called Tim on a slow pony which looked like a mini carthorse. Katy now knew what the bossy instructress was called. Her name was Val, and she was in charge of class six. Yes, just when it seemed things couldn't get much worse, they had.

Val stood in the centre of the ring, shouting, "Pompom! Pompom! Impulsion, Tim! Impulsion! Pompom! Pompom! Pompom!"

The woman's completely mad, Katy thought, stifling a giggle. This would make a brilliant comedy sketch on TV. Trouble is, it's for real and it's getting incredibly boring.

Tim had told Katy that Val was pretending to be the music because the sound system was too expensive to hire for a whole week. They were only going to have real music for the open day on Friday, when the musical ride would be performed in front of their parents.

"Tumtitum! Tumtitum! Tumtitum!" Val yelled. "Katy! Pay attention! Pompom is trotting and tumtitum is walking. How many times have I got to tell you?"

"It's a new language called gibberish, don't you know?" Tim whispered over his shoulder.

Katy snorted. "Stop it, I'm trying not to laugh as it is!"

"Stop talking, Katy!" Val screamed. "If you're not careful, I'll send you home!"

I'm going to go home anyway, Katy decided. I don't *have* to be here. It's supposed to be a fun holiday activity, not worse than school. I'll ring up Melanie this evening and ask her to come and collect me – and Trifle, of course.

"Don't go!" Alice exclaimed when Katy told her at tea time. "Mum will be so upset, after all her hard work getting us both here. I expect your mum will be too; it's a lot of money and you won't get a refund. And what about me, alone in our caravan? It won't be any fun at all without you!"

Katy knew that Alice was bound to have fun whether she was there or not – Alice was the kind of person who attracted fun and friends like a magnet – but she did see that it would appear ungrateful and rather cowardly if she left after just one day.

Alice picked up on her hesitation. "Give it one more day at least," she pleaded. "I'm sure things will get better tomorrow."

Things didn't seem to be getting any better the following morning, except the class progressed to "tarapom", which was cantering in the now official Pony Club language of gibberish.

"Tarapom! Tarapom! Change legs, Caroline! Tarapom! Tarapom!" Val yelled, on and on.

"I wonder what galloping is," Tim whispered as they lined up for one of Val's frequent lectures.

"Zoomzoom!" Katy replied. "And jumping?"

"Wheeeplop."

Katy started to laugh, and couldn't stop.

Val stood in front of Trifle. "Your sense of humour appears to be much better than your riding, Katy. I now understand why Tony said you were hopeless and needed to go right back to basics."

I'm sure Tony wouldn't have said that, Katy thought. He told me I rode very well – I'm sure he did. She felt as if she'd been punched in the stomach, and she looked down at Trifle's mane so Val wouldn't see that her eyes were blurring with tears.

"He said *my pony* needed to learn some of the basics. You see, she's only four years old. She hasn't done much work. Riding on the moor, mainly," she mumbled.

"Bad riders blame their horses," Val sneered. "Although I must admit your parents do seem to have been very foolish in buying you an Exmoor pony, of all things. And a young Exmoor at that."

"But they didn't," Katy explained. "I bought her with my own money from Brendon pony sale when she was a foal. I trained her myself."

"Well then, you have only yourself to blame,

21

haven't you?" Val said. "You're already far too big for her," she added triumphantly, and she swaggered off to her position of command in front of the class. "For the rest of the lesson we shall do some jumping," she announced.

"Wheeeplop," Tim whispered, but somehow Katy didn't find it funny anymore.

To begin with it went remarkably well – when they weren't actually jumping. Their first exercise was to trot over trotting poles in jumping position. The top classes had all the coloured show jump poles, so class six was left with rustic ones. Trifle didn't mind trotting over rustic poles; they must have looked natural, like fallen branches. She didn't even seem to mind when the last pole was raised slightly so she had to lift her legs high to trot over it, as she did when trotting through deep heather. However, once the pole became too high to trot over, she stopped in front of it and tried to go round the side. To Trifle, it probably seemed a very sensible thing to do, but Val wasn't impressed. Katy was told to try the jump again, and Val ran behind, shouting and waving her whip.

Trifle refused and then, faced with a shouting madwoman behind her, did an enormous cat-leap over the jump.

Katy was taken by surprise. She shrieked, gripped the reins to steady herself and accidentally jabbed

Trifle in the mouth. The next thing she knew, she was sitting on the ground, gasping frantically. She couldn't seem to get any air into her aching chest, and every time she tried it sounded as if someone was saying, "Hyeeee!"

"Breathe. Breathe deeply. One, two, one, two . . ." Val's bossy voice swam in and out of her consciousness.

"Are you okay, Katy?" A man's voice now – much kinder.

Katy tried to reply, but all she could manage was a long, drawn-out "Hyyyeeeee!"

"She's fine thank you, Tony. Just a bit winded, that's all. Thank you for bringing the pony back. I can't think why she galloped off to you like that."

"Perhaps she was trying to tell me something," Tony said.

"Hmm," Val replied. "Well, I think you'd better get back to your class now."

Gradually Katy's breathing eased and the pain between her ribs subsided. "I'm . . . much . . . better . . . now . . . thank . . . you," she gasped, anxious to stop Val from hovering over her.

"Good," she said. "You sit there, and I'll teach that pony of yours a lesson."

"No, please," Katy tried to protest, but Val strode up to Tim, who was holding Trifle, and started adjusting the stirrups.

As soon as Val mounted Trifle, the little pony's head shot up in alarm and her tail clamped between her legs. Katy could hardly bear to watch her looking so unhappy and frightened. She knew that what Val was doing was wrong – very wrong – but she was so weak and out of breath that she felt powerless to stop her. Val rode Trifle around the arena in trot, then canter, before heading for the jump. Trifle refused, Val whipped her, Trifle leapt over from a standstill, Val accidentally jabbed her in the mouth, Trifle stopped and was whipped, so she bucked and was whipped again.

"Don't! Please don't! She doesn't understand!" Katy tried to shout, but it came out as a breathless squeak. She couldn't believe what was happening. Her kind, beautiful, intelligent, fun-loving pony was being hurt. All the love and trust which Katy had built up with her over four years was being destroyed in a few minutes by this vicious, stupid woman. Katy scrambled to her feet and ran towards them.

"She'll be better this time! Watch and learn!" Val yelled as she cantered around Katy, turned for the jump a second time and urged Trifle to go faster by making what she must have thought were encouraging clicking noises with her tongue.

"Don't do that! She'll think it means stop so you can . . ." Katy started to shout, but it was too late.

Trifle did a spectacular sliding stop and dropped her head to the ground so her rider could dismount down her neck, but it was so abrupt that Val was catapulted into the air and hit the ground with a dull thud.

Katy hurried over and caught Trifle, while Tim and several others rode off to get help.

Tony and Mrs Edwards, the District Commissioner, soon hurried into the arena.

"Well done, everyone," Mrs Edwards said, looking flustered despite her bright and breezy smile. "I'm sure everything will be fine, but I'm afraid your lesson will have to finish early. Take your mounts back to the stables, give them a feed and a rub-down and then clean your tack. An instructor will be with you shortly." Then she hurried over to Tony, who was crouching beside Val.

Katy and Tim walked up the hill to the stables without speaking. It's odd, Katy thought, but it's much easier to find things to say when you're not supposed to be talking, like in a riding lesson, than when you can talk freely, like now.

The silence was broken by the wail of an ambulance. They turned, and saw it drive across the field towards the arena.

"Must be serious," said Tim.

Katy was shocked to realise she didn't really care.

She put a comforting hand on Trifle's neck as she jogged by her side, wild-eyed and sweaty.

At lunch, Katy was the centre of attention. Everyone wanted to know what had happened. She relayed the story over and over again, feeling slightly guilty about the thrill she felt in telling it. They were just queuing for a pudding of jelly and tinned peaches when Mrs Edwards rang the hand bell which signalled for everyone to be silent.

"Good afternoon, everyone."

"Good afternoon, Mrs Edwards," they all replied.

"As you all know, there was a slight mishap this morning. However, the good news from the hospital is that Val Smith isn't seriously hurt. She's concussed, so they'll keep her in overnight, but they're hoping to discharge her tomorrow."

"I bet they are. They'll want to get rid of her as soon as possible," Tim whispered to Katy.

"Shh!" she whispered back, smiling.

"I'm afraid we'll have to re-shuffle the classes a bit now we're short of an instructor," Mrs Edwards continued. "So, as classes three and four have the fewest riders in them, they will be amalgamated and taught by Anne Ruddock."

The female members of class four groaned rather

too loudly. Katy felt sorry for Anne Ruddock, who must have heard them. She was a good teacher, but she was a middle-aged woman, not a gorgeous young man.

"And Tony Burrell will teach class six."

Katy and her classmates beamed and whispered things like "Brill!" and "Hurray!"

The final three days sped by. Camp was just as Katy had hoped it would be, with enjoyable lessons where she and Trifle learned a lot, interesting talks from a vet and a farrier, and lots of fun in the evenings with her friends.

It was generally agreed that the performance by class six was the most entertaining demonstration at the open day. To begin with it was like a normal musical ride, with the horses and ponies walking, trotting and cantering in the formations they'd learned at the beginning of the week – although, to everybody's relief, it was all set to stirring military music rather than Val's improvisations. Then the music changed to the song *Crazy Horses*, the riders lined up, took off their jackets and ties, and things became much more interesting. Everyone was given the chance to do something he or she was good at. Caroline and Jill did a vaulting demonstration, Tim rode his pony perfectly without a saddle or bridle – he said he usually rode like that at home, and his pony certainly looked much happier for it – another boy called Charles shot arrows at a target with pinpoint accuracy while riding his pony, and Katy and Trifle demonstrated their gate-opening skills with a pretend gate Tony had made especially for them. As the smiling riders lined up to take a bow after the grand finale, Katy and Trifle walked forward a few paces. Katy clicked her tongue and Trifle lowered her head to the ground, as if she were taking a bow, to delighted applause from the audience.

Afterwards they had a prize-giving. Claire won the prize for the cleanest tack, Tim won the prize for the most improved rider and Trifle won the prize for the most improved pony. Katy knew she should have been thrilled that Trifle had won a rosette, but as she shook Mrs Edwards' hand and thanked her, she couldn't help thinking it was partly a consolation prize.

3

Competition Mix

Trifle was obviously delighted to see Jacko again and to be back in her field with sweet summer grass to eat. Katy was so tired after camp that she slept for most of Saturday, but by Sunday she was feeling much better. Her mum made her spend half the morning sorting out the great pile of belongings and dirty washing she'd brought back with her, but then she managed to escape outside for a quick ride.

"Don't be too long!" Mum called after her. "Remember, it's a family roast today."

Katy's family always called a roast dinner for all the family "a family roast", and she hadn't really thought it was odd until Alice said it sounded as if they were going to roast a member of the family. "Okay," she said. "I'll just ride Trifle up to the Common and back."

There was something different about Trifle. She was still friendly and did her best to please, but her sparkle had gone. Perhaps she's just sleepy, Katy hoped as she urged her pony up the field. After all, I'm pretty tired after camp. But in her heart she knew it was more than that. At camp Trifle had discovered that some people weren't to be trusted, and Katy was furious with herself for letting that happen. I should have relied on my instincts and taken Trifle home after the first day, she thought. She felt heavy with sadness.

Sunday lunch turned out to be a celebration, because Katy's Auntie Rachel announced that she and her husband, Mark, were going to have a baby. Katy was sitting between Granfer and Rachel at the dinner table.

"This will mean big changes for you, my girl," Granfer said to Rachel. "You won't be able to work all hours at the Exford Stables any more, will you?"

"No, but the owners want to keep me on as the manager, which is great. They've agreed to employ a groom to do a lot of the routine work like exercising the horses and mucking out. I put an advertisement in *Horse and Hound* last week, and there's been a tremendous response. They all seem to be so well-qualified, though. Most of them have degrees!"

"Sign of the times, I'm afraid," Granfer replied. "But, in my experience, qualifications are far less important than commitment for a job like that. A person's really got to love horses to look after them well."

Rachel smiled. "That's uncanny! I put *commitment more important than qualifications* and *love of horses essential* in the advert."

Granfer looked pleased. "Ha! I've taught you well, my girl!" He turned to take a dish of roast potatoes which was being handed around.

"Will you still be able to keep Moon at the stables?" Katy asked.

"Yes, so that's one less thing to worry about," Rachel replied.

"Good, I'm glad. Horses hate change, don't they? And he's had enough changes to last him a lifetime!" Katy said. Moon was Rachel's horse, and she adored him. He'd been stolen when Rachel and Mark were in Australia, but Katy, Alice, Melanie and Trifle had managed to rescue him from a dealer's yard and bring him home before he was sold. When they'd found him he'd been in a terrible state, but with loving care and good summer grass he was looking sleek and happy again.

Rachel sighed. "Oh dear, I feel so guilty about abandoning Moon when I went to Australia. He trusted me, and I let him down."

"That's just how I feel about Trifle," said Katy. "I should never have let Val ride her."

"I'd love to meet that woman and give her a piece of my mind," Granfer said.

"And we'd all like to be there when you do, Dad! Anyway, Katy, you needn't worry about her teaching at Pony Club again. Mrs Edwards told me she's not going to have anything more to do with Val and she bitterly regrets letting her teach at camp. She only recruited her at the last minute because she was short of an instructor. Val seemed to have taught at a lot of other Pony Clubs before she moved to Exmoor this year, but it turns out she upset a lot of them too."

"Oh, it's so unfair that she picked on Trifle! It's really knocked her confidence, Rachel. She was so trusting before," Katy said. "She's changed, and I don't know how I can get her back to how she was."

"Tell you what, we'll go and take a look at her after lunch, shall we?"

"Yes, please!" Katy replied. Rachel had been around ponies and horses all her life and, Katy reckoned, she understood them better than anyone else in the world.

Granfer changed the subject. "Heard how Greg's getting on, Rachel?"

Katy felt herself blushing, as she always did when Greg's name was mentioned. He was Mark's youngest brother, but still several years older than Katy, and she really liked him. She thought he was even more wonderful than Tony at Pony Club camp, and that was saying something. Unfortunately, he was on the other side of the world at the moment, working in Australia. The only contact she had with him was through Facebook, which was pretty useless because he hardly ever updated his page or answered messages.

"He's hopeless at keeping in touch, but the last time we heard he was skiing in the Snowy Mountains, the lucky devil," Rachel replied.

"Well, sometimes you're just plain lucky or unlucky in life, but other times you've got to make your own luck. He's a good worker and pleasant with it, which counts for a lot wherever you are in the world. We're missing his help already. It's hard to get reliable casual labour nowadays. Do you think he'll settle out there?"

"Highly likely. There are so many more opportunities, Dad, especially where farming's concerned."

Katy found she'd lost her appetite all of a sudden.

"She's still friendly!" Rachel commented as Trifle trotted over to the gate and nuzzled her affectionately. "But she's lost a lot of weight, hasn't she?"

"Trifle the supermodel!" Katy said, trying to hide how worried she was.

"Mm, somehow the words 'size zero' and 'Exmoor pony' don't go very well together, though," Rachel said. "It takes quite a lot to make an Exmoor thin."

"She worked harder than she's ever worked in her life at camp, and all the stress of Val riding her can't have helped either," Katy said, her anxiety tumbling out now. "We must have been riding for about five hours a day. Also, she was stabled all the time when she wasn't working, and she hates that. I think she feels imprisoned in a stable – it's not natural for an Exmoor pony to be kept inside, is it? All the fun seems to have been knocked out of her. Normally all I have to do to make her go faster is to think about it, but today I actually had to kick her along – I've never had to do that before! And she's too thin for showing, isn't she? I've entered her for Exford and Dunster shows, and they're on Wednesday the fourteenth of August and Friday the sixteenth – in less than two weeks! I don't know what to do!"

Rachel put her arm round Katy's shoulder and gave her a reassuring smile. "I think you'll be surprised how quickly she'll put on weight now she's back in a field eating summer grass, and she probably needs some nuts or a bit of coarse mix. That should pep her up as well."

"Okay," Katy said, feeling happier already.

"She'll soon start enjoying life again, you'll see," Rachel went on. "A few rides with Alice on open moorland should do the trick. Don't even *try* to start jumping her yet though, will you? When the showing season's over I'll help you with that, but she needs a complete break from it for a while. I'm pretty busy at the moment, but I'll come over next weekend to see how she is and go through your ridden and in-hand shows, if you like."

Katy hugged her aunt. "Oh, yes please! I need all the help I can get. Thanks, Rachel!"

The following day, Katy's older brother Tom had to go to the local agricultural suppliers to pick up a spare part for his muck spreader. Katy went with him so she could buy some feed for Trifle. She decided to buy coarse mix because it looked more appetising than pony nuts.

"Coarse mix, please," Katy said to the man at the counter.

"Which sort do you want?" The man studied the computer screen in front of him. "We've got Alfalfa Added Mix, Calming and Conditioning Mix, Competition Mix, Herbal Health Mix, Standard Mix, Stud Mix, Sustained Energy Mix, Ultra Light Slimming Mix or Veteran Mix."

Katy felt flustered. She had no idea there were so many different types of coarse mix. Trifle was being prepared for two important shows, so Competition Mix seemed the best option. "Competition Mix, please."

"How many bags?"

"How much should I feed?"

The man tapped away at his computer again. "Depends on the weight of the horse. For instance, it says here if it weighs five hundred kilos you should give it six to seven point five kilos of mix a day, depending on its body condition and work load." He turned the computer screen round to show her a crowded, complicated-looking table of figures.

Katy glanced at the queue which was building up behind her. She hadn't a clue how heavy Trifle was, and mental arithmetic wasn't her strong point at the best of times. "Um, five bags, please," she said, because it was the first number which came into her head and it seemed about right.

Trifle clearly approved of Competition Mix. She munched through the generous portion in her bucket in next to no time, so Katy gave her a smaller second helping. She also gave Jacko some, so he didn't feel left out.

*

To Katy's dismay, Trifle became more and more jumpy and bad-tempered as the week progressed. By Saturday, when they went for a ride on the Common with Alice, Trifle tried to bolt several times and nearly pulled Katy's arms out of their sockets. Worst of all, she started bucking for no apparent reason and shying at silly things which hadn't bothered her before. Katy was really worried, and thought it was all due to her bad experiences at camp.

Alice agreed. She said it was probably something like "post-traumatic stress", which was what some people got after they'd had a terrible experience of some kind.

This made Katy feel even more guilty about letting Val ride her pony. To show how sorry she was, she gave Trifle an extra large helping of coarse mix for her evening meal.

When Rachel visited Barton Farm on Sunday afternoon, Katy wasted no time in taking her to see Trifle.

"She's been ruined, Rachel. Completely ruined! So much for the most improved pony at camp award! It's just the opposite, in fact. Trifle used to be so good, but all she wants to do is buck, shy and bolt off with me now. She gets worse and worse every day. I think she's trying to pay me back for what happened at camp; she wants to hurt me as much as Val hurt her!"

"Just calm down, Katy. Ponies really don't think like that, you know. They're much more honest and straightforward than we are, and Trifle adores you – anyone can see that. Besides, you both had a great time at camp after Val left, didn't you?"

"Well, yes," Katy admitted.

"I'm sure there's a simple explanation," said Rachel. She ran her hands over Trifle's body and looked in her mouth. "I don't think she's got a sore back or problems with her teeth or anything, and she's certainly put on a lot of condition. What have you been feeding her?"

"Just grass – and a bit of coarse mix, like you said."

"Is this one of the bags?" Rachel asked, pointing to a half-empty bag leaning against the wall outside Trifle's stable."

"Yup."

Rachel had her serious face on. "And how many bag-fulls has she eaten this week?"

Katy avoided Rachel's eyes. "About two."

"When you say 'about two', do you mean nearer three and a half?"

Katy looked at the ground and scuffed her foot against some dry mud on the concrete. "Well, um, yes, I suppose so. But Jacko's had some as well."

"Oh, Katy! You are a silly ninny! Competition Mix is a high energy mix designed for horses like

Moon when they're doing eventing and things. Small native ponies like Trifle just don't need that sort of food. No wonder she's gone a bit loopy! Over-feeding often makes horses and ponies silly, a bit like drinking too much alcohol makes people do stupid things they wouldn't do normally. She wasn't trying to be naughty or hurt you – it's just that all that food blew her mind."

"But you told me to . . ." Katy started to say.

"Yes, I know I told you to feed her some nuts or a bit of coarse mix. It's my fault; I should have explained about the different types and the amount you should feed. Don't worry, I doubt if there's any harm done, but it's lucky I came over before she went completely bananas or got laminitis from too much food. We'd better put her to work and get rid of some of that excess energy, eh?"

After Katy's lesson, Rachel said, "There's no possibility of her falling asleep in front of the judges at Exford Show, anyway!"

"Oh dear, I hope she calms down before then," Katy said. "I don't want a repeat of last year!" Exford Show the previous year had been Trifle's first show, and it had been pretty disastrous for several reasons.

"She should calm down within a day or two, as long as you cut her feed right back. In fact, I'll take away this coarse mix and drop in some pony nuts instead, so you needn't stop feeding her completely." Rachel rubbed Trifle's forehead gently. "You'll be good as gold at Exford this year, won't you?"

Trifle snorted.

"D'you think that means yes, or no?" Katy asked.

Rachel smiled. "I think it means maybe!"

4

The Championship

As it turned out, Katy spent the day of Exford show at home with an ear infection which had started two days before. She was beginning to get better, helped by some medicine from the doctor, but she would still be too unwell and dizzy to ride in the show.

"It's so unfair!" Katy protested. "Why did I have to be ill? Today, of all days!"

Mum sighed. "I'm afraid life's like that sometimes. There's never a good time to be ill. It just happens and you have to deal with it, that's all you can do. At least you're on the mend now."

"On Friday it's Dunster Show," Katy said. "Oh, I do hope I'm better in time! I'll have to ride over to Stonyford tomorrow so we can get to the show ground early. Trifle's in the first class."

"I hope Melanie won't mind getting up at the crack of dawn. It's so kind of her to take you to all these events in her lorry," Mum said.

"She says she doesn't mind, and I'll do lots of extra work at Stonyford to say thank you." Katy loved working there anyway.

The Stonyford lorry arrived at Dunster Show soon after the gates opened, with three tired people in the cab and some rather sleepy horses and ponies in the back. They'd all been up since four-thirty that morning.

Katy's stomach was churning with a mixture of excitement, nerves and lack of sleep. Her ear still hurt too, and she felt rather giddy if she moved suddenly, but she didn't want to tell anyone about that, not even Alice. Having missed one show she wasn't going to miss another – especially not Dunster, which was the largest show on Exmoor. If she kept on growing like she had been recently, she'd definitely be too big to enter the ridden classes on Trifle next year.

Granfer was already in the showground, waiting

for the lorry. Katy loved her Granfer dearly, but his eagerness for Trifle to do well in the show ring didn't help her nerves one bit, especially when she remembered how they'd let him down at Exford Show the previous year. Although Barton Farm now belonged to Katy's dad, Granfer still owned the Barton herd of Exmoor ponies which ran wild on the Common above the farm, and he was a leading light in the Exmoor Pony Society.

"Beats me why the Exmoor pony classes are so early in the morning," Granfer grumbled as he walked to the show secretary's tent with Katy. "Exmoors are our native breed, yet most of their classes are over by the time the crowds arrive. What's your first class?"

"In-hand registered Exmoor mares, four years old or over, with or without a foal at foot," Katy said, reading from the catalogue. She was secretly glad that there weren't many people around. Hopefully it would give Trifle a chance to get over the excitement of the show ring before the crowds arrived.

Katy collected her number, went back to the lorry and unloaded Trifle – relieved to see that she hadn't sweated up or rubbed her tail. In fact, Trifle looked magnificent as she stepped down the ramp, head held high and ears pricked. Her coat shone like a dappled conker and, Katy thought, she looked just about as perfect as any pony could be.

"Pretty as a picture," Granfer said under his breath.

Alice, Melanie and Granfer fussed around Trifle while Katy climbed into the lorry and changed into her jodhpurs, boots, a white shirt, tie and hacking jacket, being careful not to get so much as a speck of dirt on any of them.

Katy had hoped that there wouldn't be many people in her class because it was so early in the morning, but her hopes were dashed when pony after pony entered the ring. Each was led by an enthusiastic owner who probably hadn't had a wink of sleep, just like her. We're all crazy, she thought. We could still be tucked up in bed. She shivered in the chilly early morning air.

The class took longer than expected because there were so many people in it. Katy found herself fighting to keep her eyes open as she stood in line waiting to do an individual show. Forgetting where she was for a moment, she yawned loudly. A jolly-looking woman standing next to her smiled sympathetically and stifled a yawn herself. Her mare had an adorable foal, which was being held by a young man who Katy guessed was the woman's son. Trifle was very interested in the foal; she kept whickering to it as if it were hers. She'll be a wonderful mum when she has a baby of her own, Katy thought, and yet again the image in her head of Trifle with a foal gave her butterflies.

The judge was a smart, efficient lady dressed in an

immaculate tweed suit. She spent a long time with each pony, even the ones which Katy considered wouldn't stand much of a chance. At last she arrived at the jolly-looking lady. Katy started to get nervous; Trifle would be next.

As the mare and foal were led out of the line so the judge could inspect them, Trifle tried to follow. When Katy held her back she whinnied, pawed the ground, circled around Katy, pawed the ground, circled again and trod heavily on Katy's foot. It hurt – a lot. Her ear ached, her foot hurt, she was cold, tired and she couldn't make up her mind whether she felt rather hungry or slightly sick. *I hate showing!* Katy thought. *It's a total waste of time. This is the last show I'm taking you to, and that's final.* "Stand still!" she growled at Trifle.

Trifle stood, but her eyes followed the foal as it trotted behind its mother. Every muscle in her body seemed tense with longing. Her nostrils fluttered in welcome when the foal eventually returned to the line.

"And what's your pony called?" asked the judge.

"Trifle."

The judge smiled warmly. "What a charming name. I think I can safely say I've never met a Trifle before. Would you like to bring her out so I can take a good look at her?"

Katy led Trifle forwards.

The judge examined the pony from head to tail. "Lovely. Can you trot her up for me, please?"

To Katy's astonishment, Trifle trotted beside her beautifully. Her interest in the foal meant she looked particularly alert and intelligent but, although Katy could tell she was keen to get back to the line, Trifle didn't forget her manners and did exactly as she was asked.

"Lovely!" the judge said again when they'd completed their individual show. "Thank you so much!" She was the sort of person who could make people feel special just by smiling at them.

There were two more in the line after Katy. Then the steward asked all the competitors to walk round the ring while the judge made her final decision. Trifle jogged behind the mare and foal eagerly, eyes shining and ears pricked, and she tried to follow them into the centre when they were asked to stand in first place.

A large, dark mare was second.

Katy's eyes wandered around the ring, trying to guess who would be third.

"Pssst!" the man walking behind Katy whispered. "Go on!"

For a moment, Katy thought he wanted her to walk faster. Then she realised that the steward was trying to catch her attention. He was waving her in! Trifle was third!

"I think I can safely say I've never given a Trifle a rosette before," the judge said, smiling warmly as she handed Katy a huge yellow rosette. "Lovely pony. Simply lovely!"

To Katy's complete surprise and delight, Trifle was placed first in her other class that day, which was for ridden Exmoor mares, stallions and geldings of four years and over.

Granfer was there waiting for her as she rode out of the ring, blushing and breathless after her lap of honour. "Well done, my girl! You're both getting the hang of this showing lark now, aren't you, eh?" he said, beaming with pleasure. He ruffled Trifle's mane affectionately as he walked by her side, the limp from his accident earlier in the year all but gone in his excitement.

Katy took Trifle back to the Stonyford lorry for a well-deserved rest, and then she and Alice went off to explore the showground and buy some lunch. After some research into the food on offer, they decided to buy beef burgers from a local farm shop because they knew the farmer.

As Katy bit into hers, a dollop of onions mixed

with ketchup squirted down her white show shirt and cream-coloured jodhpurs. "Eeek!" she squealed.

"Oh, Katy, trust you!" Alice giggled. "It's just as well you haven't got any more classes today."

They were trying to clean up the worst of the mess with napkins from the stall when Katy's mum came running up.

"Mum! I thought you weren't coming! You said you'd be too busy with the bed and breakfast guests," Katy exclaimed.

"Yes, I know, but then Granfer phoned and said you'd be in the championship, so Dad and I felt we couldn't miss that for the world," Mum replied. "Thank goodness I've found you – we've been looking for you everywhere! The competitors for the championship have just been called to the collecting ring. Hurry!"

"What championship?" Katy asked through a mouthful of burger.

"The ridden mountain and moorland championship, of course! Did no one tell you about it? The first and second prize-winners from all the ridden mountain and moorland classes are entered. Do hurry! Ugh! What on earth is that on your jods?"

"My burger hasn't behaved very well," Katy said. She made the mistake of looking at Alice, and they both collapsed into helpless laughter.

"It looks as if the burger isn't the only one!" Mum

said, looking heavenwards. "Now run, or you'll be late for the championship! Run!"

Granfer and Melanie had groomed Trifle and tacked her up. Melanie took one look at Katy's jodhpurs and told her there was a spare pair belonging to Alice in the lorry. They were uncomfortably tight, because Alice was taller and thinner, but somehow Katy squeezed into them.

"They'll have to do," she said, jumping stiffly from the lorry. "I've left the popper undone, but my hacking jacket's hiding everything."

The ponies in the collecting ring were a funny mixture of shapes and sizes, from a Shetland pony on a leading rein to a massive Highland pony with a flowing mane and tail. Katy felt unprepared and flustered as she joined them. Trifle seemed on edge too, snorting warily at the immaculate hindquarters of a large dapple grey pony in front of them. Katy guessed it was a Connemara.

"Don't worry, Trifle," whispered Katy. "I'm sure a beautiful bottom like that will be much too well-mannered to kick you. We'll never win a prize against this lot, so let's just try to enjoy ourselves."

The rider of the dapple grey turned to talk to a man standing by the collecting ring, and Katy suddenly understood why Trifle was worried. The rider was Val!

Katy felt dizzy and a bit queasy. I could leave now, she thought. I could say I don't feel well. It was true enough. But a voice inside her seemed to say, "Don't you see? This is your big chance! Your chance to show Val that she can't intimidate you. She's not your teacher any more. Now you can compete on equal terms. You can show her how good Trifle really is. It's an opportunity that's too good to miss, isn't it? You owe it to Trifle."

Determination flowed through Katy like a surge of electricity as she followed the dapple grey into the main arena. Trifle seemed to pick up her thoughts and energy – or perhaps they'd come from Trifle in the first place? Sometimes Katy wondered.

The loudspeaker crackled into life, and each pony in the championship was introduced in turn.

". . . the champion Connemara gelding Crestwood Combe Silver Shadow, owned by Mr and Mrs Tappett and ridden by Valerie Smith . . . the champion Exmoor mare Barton Trifle, owned and ridden by Katy Squires . . ."

Val's head whipped round to stare at them, a look of utter disbelief on her face. Katy held her gaze defiantly.

The riders were asked to walk, trot and canter around the ring, following each other. Then they returned to walk and the judge made his preliminary choice as, one by one, the riders were asked to line up in the centre of the ring. Katy made sure she was paying attention, but it was difficult to ride really well, look ahead, arrange her face in a serene smile and keep a close eye on the steward while pretending not to look at him.

Val was beckoned in first.

The little girl on the Shetland pony was second.

To her delight, Katy was called in third. She imagined the rosettes on her bedroom door at home: two yellow thirds with one red first in the middle. "Don't count your chickens before they're hatched, my girl," she could hear Granfer saying in her head.

The sequence of events in the show ring was becoming familiar to her now. The ponies stood in a line and the judge inspected each in turn, asked a few questions and then requested an individual show.

Val's show was perfect, as far as Katy could see.

Unfortunately, the Shetland was in a bad mood. His ears were back, and he tried to buck as he was led away from the line. Katy felt very sorry for his young rider, who smiled bravely although there were tears in her eyes.

Soon the judge was standing in front of Trifle. He was a tall, thick-set man wearing a suit and bowler hat – the sort of person, Katy decided, who wouldn't think much of Exmoor ponies. There was no small-talk about names and things, as there had been with the two lady judges earlier in the day.

In her mind Katy said, "This is it, Trifle! This is our chance to show Val how wrong she was!" She felt her pony gather herself up like a dressage horse as she set off to perform her well-rehearsed individual show. It seemed that the whole world was watching them and holding its breath. Trifle was giving the performance of her life and was thoroughly enjoying every minute of it. Katy forgot about her aching ear, her sore foot and her tight jodhpurs. She even forgot about Val as she became totally absorbed in riding; doing her very best; doing justice to her generous, forgiving pony.

"What a wonderful pony! I bet you have a lot of fun on her, don't you?" the judge said when Katy had finished.

"Yes, sir!" Katy replied. Her smile was no longer serene as she returned to her place by the Shetland in a haze of happiness. "The judge thinks you're wonderful and so do I!" she whispered to Trifle.

Most of the individual shows seemed faultless. How on earth would the judge make his final decision?

The riders were sent to walk round the ring again. Katy's heart was pounding. She knew Trifle had done her best, and that was all that mattered. Val would win

– there was no question – but it would be brilliant to be in the first five.

Granfer, Rachel, Mum, Dad, Melanie and Alice were all standing together at the ringside. Katy couldn't resist making a funny face at them as she rode past, but they didn't laugh and smile; they pointed frantically at the centre of the ring.

"Look at the steward, Katy!" Rachel hissed.

Katy looked at the steward. He seemed to be beckoning her, but she didn't know why. Perhaps her jods had split and she hadn't realised. She rode towards him anxiously.

"Congratulations! You've won the championship!" the steward said. "Could you please stand over there, starting a line in the same way as before?"

Katy often became rather deaf after a ear infection, and she wondered if she'd misunderstood him, so she said, "Sorry, I'm afraid I didn't quite hear you."

"You've won the championship. Please stand over there," the steward said clearly.

"Are you sure?"

He looked amused. "Absolutely sure. The judge has made his final decision."

"Wow! Thank you! Thank you *so much!*" Katy exclaimed, forgetting to be calm and dignified. She took up her place, bursting with pride. Out of the corner of her eye she could see her family and friends hugging each other and jumping up and down.

Val was called in second. Katy could feel rage radiating from her like heat from a fire as her pony stood next to Trifle.

This time Katy had a rosette and a large silver cup to hold as Trifle cantered round the ring in a lap of honour.

Granfer, Rachel, Mum, Dad, Melanie and Alice were at the ringside waiting for them.

"Well, what do you think of showing now, young lady?" Granfer asked.

Katy grinned. "It has its moments!"

Trifle was patted, stroked, hugged and kissed.

"She must be wondering what all the fuss is about," Katy said. "She went round in circles for hours at camp, and no one made a fuss of her. Here, she just has to do a few laps of the ring and a little show, and everyone thinks she's marvellous."

"Yes, humans are most peculiar, aren't they?" Alice said, giving Trifle yet another hug.

"Hush!" said Melanie.

The sound of Val's rasping voice could be heard above the general showground noise. Still sitting on the Connemara, she was telling the judge he was incompetent and a lot more besides.

The judge, red in the face from suppressed fury, had at last managed to interrupt Val. "If you must know, madam, the reason I chose the Exmoor mare over your pony is that the Exmoor is an excellent example of her breed, and she was brimming with character and presence. Furthermore, she looked as if she was really enjoying herself; one could see there was a wonderful partnership between the pony and her rider. I thought your pony gave a very polished performance, but there was little joy in it. He gave the impression he was working for you because he had to, not because he wanted to."

"I have never been so insulted in all my life! I will make an official complaint!" Val shouted. Most of the people in the vicinity had stopped talking and were staring at her, but she didn't notice or didn't care. She flung her rosette onto the ground and then rode to the owners, who were standing nearby and looking thoroughly embarrassed. "According to the judge, your pony doesn't have the right attitude. I'm afraid I may have to start showing for someone else," she announced. "I can't waste my time with animals which aren't going to make the grade, and if he can't win at a tin-pot little show like this there'll be no hope for him at county level."

Katy remembered one of the things Val had said to her at camp: "Bad riders always blame their horses." Now she could see the truth in it.

5

A Christmas Party

The leaves fell off the trees and the days became shorter. Almost overnight, the fields became wet and muddy. The land slipped into its annual winter sulk.

Katy's parents decided to beat the winter blues by having a Christmas party at Barton Farm. Invitations were sent out with Christmas cards at the beginning of December, and the party was set for the Saturday evening before Christmas Day.

On the day of the party each member of the family was given jobs to do. One of Katy's was to decorate the Christmas tree. When Gran and Granfer had been living at the farm she'd always helped Gran to do it, but now she was doing it by herself, mindful of the fact that Gran would cast her beady eyes over her handiwork. Carefully, Katy unravelled the lights and secured them in a spiral round the tree, starting at the top and working downwards. Oh, I forgot to check they worked, she thought, and plugged them in. Holding her breath, she switched them on. They worked, thank goodness! Next came long strands of silver tinsel, draped round the tree to hide the electric cord between the lights. Then delicate icicles of thin silver foil, which seemed to get everywhere, followed by decorations – some home-made and others bought, but most carrying a memory of some sort – and finally the fairy, which had pride of place right at the top. Katy stood back and admired the result, hoping Gran would be pleased. "It's officially Christmas!" she declared.

Her other jobs were less fun: dusting, vacuuming and helping her mum in the kitchen. Everything was ready in good time, so the family had a few minutes to sit and relax before the first guests arrived. The conversation turned to who'd been invited.

"I've asked Rachel to bring that girl who's been taken on as the groom at Exford Stables," Mum said. "Rachel thinks the world of her – says she's never known anyone work so hard."

"The horses like her too," Granfer said. "Especially Moon. She's taken to riding him quite a bit, by all accounts."

"Wow! She must be good if Rachel trusts her with Moon!" Katy remarked. "I can't wait to meet her. What's her name?"

"Sharon," said Tom. "I met her at that Young Farmers' do last weekend. She's not bad, actually, once you get over the shock of bright red hair and nose studs."

Katy giggled. "Now I *really* can't wait to meet her!"

Dean, their new neighbour, was the first to arrive. "My, what a night! Does it ever stop raining here?"

"Yes, sometimes it snows," Granfer said wryly, handing Dean a glass of mulled wine. "How are you getting on at Wellsworthy, then? I sheared my first sheep in the barn there. That was in Ted Delbridge's day, and the only power was from the waterwheel."

"Amazing! It's great hearing things like that – brings the whole place to life, somehow." Dean said. "I'd love to get that old water wheel going again one day. Could you come and give me some advice?"

"Be glad to," Granfer said.

Katy smiled to herself. Granfer was particularly

good at giving advice, whether it was asked for or not.

"And I'd like to restore those old stables underneath the bank barn as well," Dean said. "I've always fancied having a horse – don't know a thing about them, mind you. Is there anyone around here who could teach me the basics, just to get me going?"

"Melanie Gardner would teach you, I'm sure. She owns Stonyford Riding Stables. It's about a mile away. She's a good horsewoman, is Melanie," Granfer said.

"As long as she isn't one of those bossy, fussy horsy ladies. All I want to do is gallop over the moors and enjoy myself. I don't want any of that going round in circles nonsense."

Katy grinned. Melanie, Alice and the twins had arrived, and were standing right behind Dean.

Melanie had obviously heard every word, and was highly amused. "How do you do?" she said, holding out her hand. "I'm Melanie – the bossy, fussy horsy lady from Stonyford. Who are you?"

Unphased, he laughed, took her hand and said, "Pleased to meet you! I'm Dean – the tactless wannabe cowboy from Wellsworthy. I moved there last summer."

"So we're neighbours!" Melanie said, looking pleased. "How come we've never met before?"

"Probably because I'm in London most of the time,

but all that'll change next year. I've finally sold the business, so I'll be able to live down here full time."

"And what did you do in London?" Melanie asked.

"Computers – recycling computers, to be precise. I started it all up when I left school, and luckily I hit the jackpot. So now I can enjoy life, go back to my rural roots and all that. My granddad was a farmer in Yorkshire. I used to . . ."

Katy and Alice left Dean talking to Melanie, and went to say hello to Rachel. She was standing by the door with Mark.

"Hello, how's the bump?" Katy greeted her aunt.

Rachel patted her tummy. "Getting bumpier by the day. Three months to go!"

"Wow! How exciting! D'you know if it's going to be a boy or a girl?"

"No, it'll be a lovely surprise." Rachel looked behind her. "That's odd! Sharon was here with us just now, but she seems to have disappeared. What a pity, I did so want you two girls to meet her!"

"Don't worry, we'll look out for her," Katy said.

"Yes, do. She's pretty easy to spot, with her bright red hair."

A farmer who lived near Rachel and Mark started talking to them about some sheepdog puppies they had for sale, so Katy and Alice went off in search of Sharon. However, there was no sign of a girl with red hair anywhere. They even checked the loos, to make sure she hadn't accidentally locked herself in. Eventually they gave up, partly because so many guests had arrived that it was difficult to move. The roar of conversation was deafening.

"Let's go upstairs to my room!" Katy yelled in Alice's ear.

Alice gave a thumbs up sign.

I n Katy's bedroom the noise from the party filtered up through the floorboards as a low mumble of jumbled conversations interspersed with laughter. At last they could talk to each other without shouting.

Katy turned on her computer and said excitedly, "Greg sent me a message on Facebook!"

"Oooh, what did he say?" Alice asked.

"I'll show you, just a mo . . . Look, he's put: *We're having a serious drought here. Can you send some of your Exmoor rain over?*"

"That'd be funny! Why don't you?" Alice said.

"What d'you mean?"

"Why don't you send some Exmoor rain to Greg? It would be a brilliant joke present, wouldn't it?"

"Hmm, I don't know. What would I send it in?"

"A bottle or something. It would have to be plastic, so it wouldn't smash in the post."

"He might think I was being silly."

"Probably, but he'd also think it was funny, wouldn't he?"

Katy was impatient to show Alice the rest of the message. "I suppose so," she said. "Look, he goes on to say how many sheep he's shorn, plus they've been rounding up cattle with helicopters – how cool is that? And then he's put *Happy Christmas to everyone at Barton Farm, love from Greg.* He wrote *love from Greg!* Isn't that great? I mean, he could have just put best wishes or something, couldn't he?"

Alice jumped onto Katy's bed and sat with her back against the wall. "I suppose so, but perhaps you shouldn't read *too* much into it. He's probably just being friendly in an older brother sort of way. I mean, he *is* a lot older than you, and . . ."

"Only ten years older," Katy protested. "Dad married Mum, and he's nine years older than she is."

"Wow, you want to *marry* him?"

"Well, maybe. When I'm a lot older, of course. When I'm twenty and he's thirty, perhaps."

"What if he stays out in Australia?"

"I wouldn't mind living there. We could have a house on stilts with a veranda, like the one in this photo – that's where he's working at the moment – and we'd have lots of horses and dogs."

"And I could be your bridesmaid!"

62

"Of course!"

A mischievous look came over Alice. She wriggled off the bed again and ran to the computer. "I think we'd better tell Greg about our plans, don't you?" she said, pretending to type on the keyboard.

"Alice! Don't you *dare!*" Katy cried out, pulling her away.

They tripped over each other, and ended up sprawled on the floor, giggling and struggling. Suddenly, Katy caught sight of what appeared to be two eyes staring at her from under her bed. She screamed.

"Sssh! Be quiet, for goodness sake!" the eyes said. They had a strong Irish accent. "I'll come out as long as you're quiet, okay?"

Katy and Alice clung to each other. "Okay," they both said in turn.

A thin, dishevelled girl with bright red hair and nose studs appeared. Katy was embarrassed to see how much dust she'd picked up from under the bed.

"We've met you before, haven't we?" said Katy, recognising her instantly.

The girl dusted herself off as best she could and sat down on Katy's bed. "Yes, I'm afraid you have." She put her head in her hands. "Oh dear, what a mess!" she wailed. "Rachel will *kill* me when she finds out!"

"What on earth are you talking about?" Alice asked, looking from the girl to Katy and back again.

"This is Sharon," Katy said. "Don't you remember? She's the girl who was working in that dealer's yard when we rescued Moon. She rode him over that awful jump, and gave us his real passport as we were leaving."

"Of course! You rode with trainers and no hat – Mum was horrified!" Alice exclaimed. Then, realising she'd said the wrong thing, she added, "But we all thought you rode really well."

"Yes, and we felt awful leaving you to cope with everything after the police took that crooked dealer away," Katy said.

Sharon looked up. The makeup round her eyes had smudged, which made her look even more gaunt. "The dealer's my uncle – the only family I have," she said.

"Oh, I'm really sorry. What happened to the rest of your family?" Alice asked, typically direct.

"Alice!" Katy whispered

"It's okay, I don't mind telling you. It's a pretty depressing story, though," Sharon said. "First, can you get some food? It smells lovely and I'm starving."

When most people said they were starving it was merely an expression, but in Sharon's case it seemed a real possibility. Her angular frame was visible under her tunic top, and her limbs weren't much thicker than the bones which supported them.

"Good idea, I'm hungry too," Katy said. "I'll be back in a minute."

Mum was busy in her not-so-new kitchen, ladling out mulled wine and keeping a constant supply of party food on the go. Plates of food ready to be handed around jostled for space with used glasses and dishes waiting to be washed up. At first glance it looked as if there'd been some sort of catastrophe, like an earthquake.

"Can I take some food and drink up to my room? Katy asked.

"Help yourself," Mum said, obviously flustered. "But don't make a mess."

Katy piled a plate high with a jumble of cocktail sausages, sandwiches, mini pizzas and mince pies, delivered them upstairs and returned for some drink. Two glasses of non-alcoholic mulled wine had been put out for her. "Can I have another?"

"Why do you want three?" Mum asked.

"Sharon's with us."

"Oh, the poor girl won't want to talk ponies with you and Alice all evening! Bring her down so she can be with Tom and other people her age."

"No, she likes it with us," Katy said, and hurried upstairs again.

They ate, drank and talked. Katy sat on the chair by her desk while Alice sat on the bed with Sharon. The noise from downstairs increased, and laughter became more frequent. Outside, rain spattered against the window. Bit by bit, Sharon told Katy and Alice her story.

Sharon had grown up in Ireland. She'd never known her father. Home had been a small caravan which she'd shared with her mother, who'd turned her hand to whatever jobs were available. She'd loved working with horses best – a passion she'd passed on to her daughter. When Sharon was twelve, her mother had been offered a job in a racing stables. It seemed their luck had changed! They had a house, Sharon went to school, they were surrounded by horses and their boss was very kind. But one icy morning, while Sharon's mother was driving into town to do some shopping, a car had skidded into hers and she'd been killed instantly. Devastated, Sharon had been left with no known relatives except her uncle in England, who'd been a jockey and was now a horse dealer. He'd given her a home, but had treated her no better than a slave. She couldn't bear the way he'd neglected the horses which were supposed to be in his care, nor the terrible lies he'd told his customers. To him, horses had been money-making units, nothing more. Sharon had tried not to get too fond of any of the animals which passed through the yard, but some had been so special she couldn't help it. Her favourite had been Moon – renamed Comet by her uncle – and Sharon had been distraught when Melanie, Katy and Alice had turned up with Mr Jackson to claim him. On the same evening, of course, her uncle had been arrested and taken away. He was now in prison and, until a few months ago, she'd been in a hostel for young people.

Katy listened intently. What would she have turned out like, she wondered, if fate had given her a similar start? A life so different from the one she had known with a loving family, a wonderful home and her own ponies? "How did you get the job in Exford Stables?" she asked.

"It was incredible good luck," Sharon replied. "You see, I had toothache . . ."

"Toothache!" Katy butted in. "I don't call that lucky!"

"Ah, but sometimes bad things lead to good things," Alice said wisely. "Think, if Granfer hadn't had his accident, you and Trifle wouldn't have rescued him, you wouldn't have met the film crew and they wouldn't have seen your dad's paintings."

"Sounds as if you've got some much better stories to tell *me*," Sharon said.

"Ours are only better because they all seem to have happy endings," Katy replied.

"I thought mine did until I came here this evening," Sharon said wistfully.

"Please finish it, and we'll do our best to give it a happy ending," said Katy.

"Well, okay. But I don't see how, unless you can work miracles," Sharon replied. She told them how she'd picked up a copy of *Horse and Hound* in the dentist's waiting room, and had seen Rachel's advertisement for a groom. She'd got on well with Rachel from the start and, to her amazement, she got the job! She'd been so happy working with Rachel at the stables, and within a few days she'd realised that Moon was the horse she'd known as Comet at her uncle's yard – though now, of course, he looked much better. Hoping her secret would never be discovered, she'd decided not to say anything about it to Rachel for fear of losing her job. Everything had seemed to be going well until that evening, when she'd walked into the sitting room and recognised Melanie, Alice and Katy. In a panic, she'd bolted upstairs and hidden in Katy's room.

The girls were just discussing how to tell Rachel about Sharon's past when there was a knock on the door and Rachel's voice said, "Sharon? Are you in there? Are you okay?"

Katy opened the door. "Come in and join the alternative party," she said. "Guess what? It's a tremendous coincidence, but . . ." and she told Rachel a short version of Sharon's story. When she'd finished, she said, "Sharon was afraid you'd be angry with her, but I told her you wouldn't be. I'm right, aren't I?"

Rachel smiled, and hugged Katy. Then she hugged

Sharon. "Of course I'm not angry with you," she said. "After all, you've done nothing wrong; it was your uncle who was the crook. And I'm certainly not going to fall out with the best groom on Exmoor! Just promise me one thing."

"Anything," Sharon said happily.

"No more secrets. If you think there's something I ought to know, tell me. Okay?"

"I promise. No more secrets."

"Hurray! A happy ending!" Katy exclaimed.

Having been the first to arrive, Dean was one of the last to leave, along with the Gardners.

It was still pouring with rain. Katy and her family sheltered in the porch as they waved goodbye to the departing cars.

"Melanie seemed to get on very well with Dean, didn't she?" Mum commented.

"You're telling me!" Dad said. "I don't think she talked to anyone else for the whole evening."

"I heard him arranging riding lessons," Tom added. "Sounds serious!"

Serious for the poor horse who has to put up with his hit-pats, anyway, Katy thought, although she had to admit she was beginning to like Dean. She waited until everyone else had gone back inside. Then she took a small plastic bottle from the recycling bin, washed it thoroughly and filled it with pure rainwater from Barton Farm. On Monday morning she went into town with her mum, for some last-minute Christmas shopping, and posted the bottle to Greg in Australia. Nancy in the Post Office was puzzled by the customs label Katy stuck to the parcel:

DESCRIPTION OF GOODS: RAIN (GIFT)
VALUE OF CONTENTS: PRICELESS

6

Home Alone

Katy checked the post and her emails every day, expecting news that Greg had received his unusual Christmas present, but there was no word from him.

Soon it was the end of January, when Mum and Dad were going to London for a week's holiday. In fact, as they kept reminding everyone, it was for pleasure *and* business because some of Dad's paintings had been chosen for a special exhibition of modern landscape artists in a smart London gallery.

They left on a cold, wet Sunday morning.

"Goodbye, darling," Mum said, hugging Katy. She

smelt of town clothes and the scent she only usually wore for parties. "I've put a note on the table to remind you about everything you'll have to do. The fridge is well-stocked and there's lots of food in the freezer. Make your packed lunch for school the night before and store it in the fridge. Tom will take you down to the bus stop, won't you, Tom?"

Tom nodded. "Don't worry," he said in a low, dependable-sounding tone of voice.

"Take care of each other, now. Remember, we're only a phone call away," Mum said, hugging Katy and Tom in turn.

Dad kissed Katy and gave Tom a fatherly pat on the shoulder. "Bye, Tom. Remember to check the cows regularly – one or two are very close to calving. Oh, and please fence round those silage bales in Moor Field. I'm sorry to go on about it, but you really should have done it in the autumn. It's an accident waiting to happen."

"Yeah, yeah, Dad. I said I'll do it, and I'll do it, okay?" Tom said.

"Well, make sure you do. Good luck with everything, both of you, and no silly arguments!" Dad said. Then he and Mum got into the car and drove off, waving.

*

To begin with, Katy thought being alone with Tom was great fun. They made toasted sandwiches for lunch and ate them in the sitting room, watching television. Mum never allowed her family to eat in the sitting room.

There was a good film on television, and they watched all of it. Afterwards, it was a mad dash to get all the livestock fed and watered before nightfall. At least there were no stables to muck out; neither Jacko nor Trifle were clipped, so they didn't have to be stabled at night.

Katy still had her homework to do after the farm work was finished. Whatever her good intentions, she usually left homework until the last minute.

"We'll have a proper fry-up for tea," Tom said. "I'll cook and you can wash up."

By the time she'd finished her homework, she was too tired to wash all the dirty dishes and greasy, charred pans in the sink.

Katy overslept on Monday morning. Mum usually woke her if she overslept, but Mum wasn't there. She raced downstairs. The house was empty. It appeared Tom had gone out to do the farm work, forgetting he was supposed to drive Katy to the bus stop.

There was no time for breakfast, and Katy hadn't remembered to make a packed lunch. She grabbed her school bag and ran down the lane. The bus stop was almost a mile away. She arrived in the nick of time. A friend gave her a sandwich and a bit of chocolate at lunch time but, apart from that, she had nothing to eat all day.

Tom wasn't at the bus stop after school either, so Katy had to walk home in the wind and rain. It was nearly dark and she didn't have a torch. She was cold, hungry and miserable by the time she reached Barton Farm. Dashing into the kitchen, she grabbed some biscuits, put the kettle on and huddled up to the Aga, shivering.

Tom walked in. "Oh good, you've put the kettle on. Cup of tea, please," he said.

Katy's anger, which had been simmering, came to the boil. "Get it yourself," she snapped. "I nearly missed the bus this morning, thanks to you!"

"Sorry, but there was a cow calving and I had one hell of a job getting the calf to suck," Tom said. "I completely forgot about your bus, to be honest."

"What about this evening, then? Another cow calving? It was pouring, and I'm soaked to the skin!"

"No need to tell me about the weather – I've been working in it all day. Look, I'm sorry I forgot, but after all the problems this morning I got behind with the rest of the work, okay?"

"No, not okay," Katy replied. "I'm off to have a bath and warm up. What's for supper?"

"Whatever you feel like cooking," came the reply.

"I hope you fenced off those silage bales, like Dad asked you to," Katy shouted over her shoulder as a parting shot, knowing full well that Tom wouldn't have.

As Katy lay in the steaming bath, she heard the wind whistling around the house and slates rattling on the roof. It was going to be a stormy night.

On Tuesday morning, Katy's alarm went off and she awoke in good time. Annoyingly, Tom also knocked on her door to wake her, but at least he was there to drive her to the school bus. An added bonus was that Katy had time to make a packed lunch.

"Wow! It must have been quite a storm last night," Katy remarked as they drove down the lane. "Look at all the branches everywhere."

"Yup," said Tom grimly. "I'm dreading going round the farm to see what damage has been done. Typical it should happen while Dad's away."

That evening, Tom wasn't there to pick Katy up from the bus. *I knew his thoughtfulness this morning was too good to last,* she said to herself as she trudged home in semi-darkness. This time, however, she had a torch.

As Katy passed by the farmyard, she noticed

Uncle Mark's tractor and silage wrapper parked there, which struck her as most peculiar. She knew that silage had to be wrapped as soon as it was made in the summer, otherwise it went mouldy. Grass hardly grew in the winter, so nobody on Exmoor made silage then.

Mark and Tom were having a cup of tea in the kitchen.

Tom swore when Katy walked in. "Sorry, I forgot again, didn't I?"

"Yes. Don't worry, I'm getting used to it," Katy said, helping herself to a cup of tea.

"You see, I had a bit of an emergency here. Mark had to come." Tom stopped abruptly, as if he realised he was saying too much.

"Slates off the roof," Mark said.

Tom looked relieved. "Yes," he said.

"So why's the silage wrapper in the yard? Did you wrap the slates in plastic?" Katy asked.

Tom laughed nervously. "Er, no. Some silage bales had rat damage, so I had to re-wrap them."

"That's odd. Dad usually patches up rat holes with silage tape. Why did you bother to re-wrap the bales?" Katy asked.

"They were big rats – lots of them. But don't worry, I've dealt with them now," Tom said in his low, dependable-sounding tone of voice.

"Oh, are you sure?" Katy didn't like the idea of Barton Farm teeming with big rats.

Mark seemed anxious to change the subject. "Coming to the skittles match on Thursday night, Tom?"

"Can't. I promised Mum and Dad I wouldn't leave Katy alone in the house at night," Tom said.

"How about getting Sharon to babysit? I'm sure she could do with a bit of extra cash, and I know she really likes Katy – couldn't stop talking about how kind she was at the Christmas party. I could drive her over here and pick you up at the same time."

"Ahem! Do I have a say in this, as the baby who's going to be sat on?" Katy asked. Her mood was lighter now she'd had some tea and a couple of biscuits.

"You wouldn't mind, would you?" Tom asked.

"No, I don't mind at all," Katy replied, smiling sweetly. "I'd rather spend an evening with Sharon than with you any day of the week! It's just nice to be asked, that's all." Sensing she ought to quit while she was ahead in the never-ending game of one-upmanship she had with her brother, she drank the rest of her tea and said, "I'm going out to see the ponies once I've changed out of my school things."

"Er, they're in a different field tonight. They escaped last night – it looks as if the gate was damaged in the storm – so I put them in Lane Meadow for now," Tom said.

"Oh dear. They didn't injure themselves at all, did they?"

"No, they're absolutely fine. No harm done," Tom said in his low, dependable-sounding tone of voice.

Why do I smell a rat? Katy wondered as she went upstairs to get changed. Not the kind of rat that eats silage, either.

She hurried out to see Trifle and Jacko, and was relieved to find that Tom seemed to be right: they were absolutely fine.

On Thursday night, Mark delivered Sharon to Barton Farm and picked up Tom.

Sharon walked into the kitchen and exclaimed, "Ugh! Gross! Don't you ever do any washing-up?"

"No," Tom said cheerfully as he was leaving. "But we'll have to soon because we're running out of clean dishes. Bye then, you girls. Be good!"

"Right!" Sharon said to Katy. "I'll wash, and you can dry everything and put it away."

"But Tom made most of this mess! I don't see why I should clear up all his dirty dishes!" Katy complained.

"Well, I'm not responsible for any of this, but I'm going to do it because it needs to be done," said Sharon.

"If you don't want to help, fine. Go and watch TV or something."

Katy knew she couldn't leave Sharon to do the washing-up while she did nothing, so she took a cloth from the drawer and walked over to the sink.

Soon, the girls were chatting like old friends.

"When's your mum coming back?" Sharon asked.

"Sunday lunchtime."

"She mustn't come home to a mess. If I can get a lift over here on Sunday morning, I'll come and help you tidy up before she gets home."

"Could you, Sharon? That would be great!" Katy said. "Somehow, all this cleaning isn't as bad when there's two of us. It seems so impossible by myself. I'm beginning to realise how much work Mum does."

True to her word, Sharon went to Barton Farm on Sunday morning to help Katy clean the house. With Sharon there, Tom decided to help too. When they'd finished the housework, they all went down to the farmyard and tidied that up as well. Working with Sharon made any job seem easier.

After lunch, Sharon left and Katy went for a quick ride up to the Common on Trifle. She was amazed to see that Tom had fenced round the silage bales in Moor Field at last. On closer inspection she guessed, from the tractor tyre marks in the mud around them, that they were the bales which had been re-wrapped due to rat damage. In between the tyre marks, though, Katy was sure there were traces of hoof-prints. Intrigued, she rode to the Common gate. Sure enough, the mud around the gate was thick with hoof-prints. Katy felt like an ace detective solving a crime. The whole herd of Exmoor ponies must have broken in from the Common and ripped open the silage bales! No wonder Tom didn't want her to know – Dad had been warning him something like that would happen if the bales weren't fenced off to protect them, and he'd been proved right. The ponies had been the "big rats". So *that* was Tom's secret! She'd store it up, in case it proved useful at a later date.

M um and Dad were delighted to see how clean and tidy everything was on their return.

"We'll have to go away more often!" Mum said.

"Please don't!" Katy replied. Life was much easier when packed lunches, lifts to the bus, clean clothes and washing-up just happened like magic.

7

The Lesson

At the beginning of March, the vet said that Jacko could be shod and ridden again. Katy rode Jacko in a field to begin with, just in case he'd turned wild after so much time off. She needn't have worried; he was as dependable as ever. She'd become so used to Trifle's round body, bushy mane and short, quick strides that it felt really strange to be riding Jacko again. In many ways, she admitted to herself, it was a huge relief. With Jacko she could relax and enjoy the ride, whereas with Trifle she was acutely aware of her pony's inexperience. Trifle still had a lot to learn, and it was up to Katy to teach her in the right way. She felt that intense responsibility every time she rode her.

Added to this, Jacko seemed to be delighted he was being ridden again. Katy had always assumed that any horse or pony, if given the choice, would prefer to laze around and graze all day rather than working. The idea that Jacko might have been bored with nothing to do – or could even have thought he'd done something wrong and nobody wanted to ride him anymore – had never occurred to her before. I wish I knew more about horses, she thought. I mustn't let Trifle feel neglected now I'm riding Jacko again.

She told Alice about Jacko when she rang her that night.

"Brill!" Alice said. "You'll soon be in the Pony Club jumping team, you wait and see!"

"I bet I've forgotten how to jump!" Katy said. But she had to admit it was thrilling to imagine jumping with Jacko again, and being in the same group as Sophie and Fiona at Pony Club, and also, perhaps, being picked for a team.

Sharon now spent a lot of her spare time at Barton Farm. She was always welcome and always made herself useful. She helped Mum in the house, Tom on the farm and Katy with Trifle and Jacko.

On the Sunday after Jacko had been shod, Katy and Sharon decided to go for a ride on the two ponies. The weather was perfect: sunny, fresh and clear, with enough clouds to make the sky interesting but too few to make it cloudy. As they set off up the fields towards the Common, the ponies seemed overjoyed to be together for a change. They showed off to each other, arching their necks and prancing like high-class dressage horses.

"I think Jacko will explode if I don't let him go faster," Katy said when they got into Moor Field. "Shall we trot up to the Common gate?"

"Okay by me," Sharon replied.

So Katy set off across the field at a trot, then an extended trot, then a canter. When they reached the gate, she turned to Sharon and said, "Sorry, I couldn't resist it."

Sharon giggled. "That's fine. It's such fun to be riding a pony again, although compared with Moon she's a bit like a sewing machine!"

Katy laughed. "Poor Trifle! I know exactly what you mean, though. Her little legs have to move so fast to keep up." She opened the gate onto the Common and closed it again once they were through. "That's where Trifle and I first met, on my birthday nearly five years ago," she said, pointing to a circle of gorse nearby. "It was terrible weather and she'd only just been born. I think she mistook me for her mother, because she came right up to me. She was so thin and weak; she nearly didn't survive." Katy looked at her pony and smiled. "Now look at her! Hard to imagine, isn't it?"

"Certainly is," Sharon agreed, stroking Trifle's neck. "So you share the same birthday?"

"Yup. I knew from the moment I saw her that we'd share our lives too. It was meant to be, somehow."

"You're a lucky girl, Katy Squires!" Sharon said. "Sometimes I thought things were meant to be in my life, but it turned out they weren't – like Mother's job at the racing stables."

"Sorry, I feel guilty about saying that now, but it hasn't all been easy." As they rode along, Katy told Sharon about Trifle failing her inspection, buying her back at Brendon pony sale and keeping her at Stonyford. She also told her how the farm was nearly sold and how Granfer was rescued after his accident. "So you see," she said, "I think Granfer's right: sometimes you're just plain lucky or unlucky in life, but other times you've got to make your own luck. Like you did, Sharon." Katy grinned. "You got that job as a groom, and because of that you met me!"

Sharon laughed. "Is that lucky or unlucky?"

Katy leaned down and gave Sharon a pretend punch. "Will you be offended if I tell you something?"

Sharon looked amused. "Why do people ask that

before they say something really offensive? Go on."

"When Alice and I first saw you at your uncle's yard in Tiverton, we thought you were really . . . um . . . weird and grumpy, but we didn't know anything about you, did we? I like you a lot now. I wish I had a big sister like you."

"Well, I've always wanted a sister myself, so perhaps we should adopt each other," said Sharon. "And will you be offended if I tell you something?"

"Why do people ask that before they say something really offensive? Go on!" Katy replied, mimicking Sharon's Irish accent.

"When I saw you for the first time, I thought you were a stuck-up snob, with that posh lorry and your fancy riding gear," said Sharon. "But I didn't know anything about you, either. It just goes to show that you shouldn't judge people by appearances, doesn't it?"

Katy agreed. She spotted a long, low gorse bush nearby, just waiting to be jumped. "D'you mind if I jump that?" she asked. "It's ages since I've jumped anything with Jacko, and I'm longing to start again. You'd better go round it, though, because Trifle's afraid of jumping."

Jacko jumped the gorse willingly, and Katy let out a whoop of joy. She glanced behind her just in time to see Trifle leaping over the same bush with her ears pricked, giving Jacko a rumbling whinny as if to say, "Wait for me!"

"Wow! A jumping sewing machine! She was so eager to keep up with you that I decided to let her have a go. I hope you don't mind," said Sharon, giving Trifle a light pat on the neck.

"Why should I mind? I'm really pleased!" Katy replied. "She looked as if she really enjoyed it. I was anxious about giving her some proper jumping lessons, but perhaps she'll learn more like this, when she doesn't even realise she's having a lesson. Shall we try it again?"

They soared over the gorse bush, side-by-side this time.

"Again?" Katy asked gleefully.

"I'd love to but, as your new-found sensible older sister, I think we should leave it on a good note," Sharon replied. "Jacko's not fit yet and I don't want Trifle to get too excited."

They walked on in companionable silence.

Katy allowed her thoughts to turn to Greg. Ever since she'd sent that stupid bottle of rainwater to Australia she hadn't heard from him. A few weeks ago she'd plucked up the courage to send him an email asking if he'd received his Christmas present, because it could have been lost in the post. There'd been no reply, and Katy didn't dare to send another in case he thought she was being a pest. She hadn't told anyone about her predicament – not even Alice, who'd given her the idea in the first place – but now it felt right to ask Sharon's advice. "Um, have you ever had a boyfriend?" she asked shyly.

Sharon looked amused. "A few," she replied. "But none of them turned out to be worth the bother. How about you?"

"No, but . . ." Katy felt foolish all of a sudden. Why on earth had she started this conversation?

"But Mark's younger brother, Greg, is in Australia at the moment, and you really like him?" Sharon asked. She didn't look amused any more, just sympathetic.

"How do you know?" Katy asked. She could feel her cheeks burning.

"I was hiding under your bed when you and Alice were talking about him in your room, remember? I didn't mean to eavesdrop but I couldn't help it."

"Oh, no!" Katy exclaimed, remembering every word they'd said, including their ridiculous wedding plans.

"Did you send him some rain in a bottle? I thought that was a great idea!" Sharon said.

"Yes, so did I," Katy replied. "I thought he'd love it, but he didn't. Shows I don't know him very well, I suppose."

"Why? What did he say?"

"That's the trouble! He hasn't said *anything* – not one word since I sent it!"

"Perhaps it got lost in the post or something," Sharon said kindly.

"I thought that to begin with, but he's not answering my emails anymore either. I've ruined everything, and all because of a silly bottle of water which I sent flying halfway round the world!"

"Well, if he's that stuffy he's probably not worth bothering about. I should leave it for now and see what happens. You can make your own luck in life, but sometimes it has the opposite effect if you try too hard. Just wait and see if it's meant to be."

"Okay, I'll try. It isn't easy, though." Katy smiled at Sharon. "Thanks."

"What for?"

"For not laughing at me – for being a good friend."

The girls were riding back over the Common when they met Melanie and Dean. Melanie was riding Max, her chestnut hunter, and Dean was on Major, the most dependable horse at Stonyford. Katy was amused to see that Major was on a leading rein; it was funny to see an adult being led. One look at Dean's riding style showed it was a wise precaution. His toes pointed downwards, which tipped his body forwards so that he had to steady himself by gripping the pommel of the saddle with his hands. This gave him no control over the reins, which hung loosely like skipping ropes.

"Howdee, Pardners! Whadda ya think?" Dean said in a mock American drawl. Katy stifled a giggle. She thought Dean was one of the worst riders she'd ever seen.

"For what it's worth, I think you're taming that mustang just fine, cowboy. But you'll find it a heck of a lot easier to stay upright if you keep your heels down," Melanie said, winking at Katy.

"Yes, Ma'am!" Dean said, sitting up in the saddle and saluting. He nearly overbalanced, and saved himself from falling off by grabbing the pommel of the saddle again.

Melanie glanced heavenwards, but Katy could see she was enjoying herself. She wasn't usually this jokey when teaching someone to ride.

"Guess what? Sharon jumped Trifle over a gorse bush, and she cleared it brilliantly!" Katy said.

"That's great news," said Melanie. "And it's lovely to see Jacko out and about again. You'll be kept busy now, with two ponies to ride."

"To a casual observer, it seems that most of the women round here are dangerously addicted to collecting horses!" Dean said.

Melanie smiled. "Sadly, it's an affliction with no

known cure. Come on, cowboy. I've got to get back to the ranch in time for the two-thirty ride. Bye, Katy. Bye, Sharon."

When Melanie and Dean were out of hearing distance, Katy said, "Crikey! Isn't Dean a terrible rider?"

"I expect you were once too. Don't you think it's good he wants to learn, though? It takes a lot of courage to try something completely new," Sharon replied.

Katy felt mean, and wished she hadn't said anything.

8

Out of the Blue

Rachel and Mark had a baby daughter on 28th March. They called her Heather. When Rachel and Heather were back from the hospital, Mum took Katy to visit them.

As soon as she walked in through the door, Katy sensed the house was different. It smelt of washing powder, and it was clean and tidy. Baby clothes hung to dry over the cooker instead of the usual muddy girths and horse bandages. Rachel was different too – strangely soft and motherly, wearing a dressing gown rather than her usual jeans and polo shirt. Katy felt very out of place, and wasn't sure what to do or say. In contrast, Mum was in her element, talking about hospitals, nappies and anything to do with babies. Heather started to cry. It was a loud, demanding cry.

Mum picked her up and gave her a cuddle. "You were once this size, Katy," she said. "Oh, I do love babies! Here you are, Rachel. I think she needs a feed."

Katy found it impossible to believe that she'd ever been like the tiny, pink, helpless bundle lying in Rachel's arms. Other baby animals, like foals and lambs, were much more fun than human babies.

Rachel smiled at Katy. "Mark and I have a very special favour to ask you," she said. "Will you be Heather's godmother? Sharon's going to be her other godmother, and Greg's agreed to be her godfather."

Katy felt speechless. She was astonished and flattered by Rachel's request, but it was the mention of Greg's name which really took her by surprise.

"How is Greg? Still in New Zealand?" Mum asked.

"No, he arrived back in Australia yesterday. All right for some, eh? Nine months' work and then three months' play. He telephoned this morning. It sounds as if he had a great time. Oh, and he loved the water you sent him, Katy! What a brilliant present! He drank a toast to Heather with it while he was on the telephone, and he said it was better than any champagne."

*

Two weeks later, a large parcel arrived for Katy from Australia. It contained a huge toy kangaroo and a postcard of a Merino sheep. On the back of the postcard, Greg had written,

Happy Birthday – well, I'm posting this on your birthday! I'm not as good at presents as you are, but I hope you like Katy the Kangaroo. Her baby (called a joey) is inside her pouch. I'm coming home for Heather's christening at the end of the year.
See you then. Give Heather a cuddle from me.
Love, Greg.

The kangaroo had pride of place on Katy's bed, and she read the postcard several times a day for the next few weeks. She felt as if she were walking on air. She wasted no time in telling Sharon about Greg's present, and she sent Alice a text about it because Alice's father had taken her and her twin brothers – together with his new wife – to the Bahamas for the whole of the Easter holidays.

"It's strange, but everything seems to be better since Greg sent me that parcel," Katy said to Sharon as they rode over the Common. This time, Katy was riding Trifle and Sharon was on Jacko.

"You mean the birds sing louder, the sun's brighter and honey tastes sweeter?" Sharon said in a jokey romantic voice.

"Okay, okay, make fun of me if you like, but it's true," Katy said. "Jacko and I have just been picked for the one day event and show jumping teams too, so there's another good thing that's happened.

They stopped to look at a mare and foal. Trifle arched her neck and snorted, then whickered softly.

"It can't be more than a few days old. Isn't it *gorgeous*?" said Sharon. "Look, Trifle wants one!"

"Yes, I know," said Katy. A thought suddenly occurred to her. "Wouldn't it be perfect if she could run out here with the herd this summer? That way, she'd have a foal next spring. I wasn't planning to set her free yet, but it would make sense, wouldn't it? I mean, she obviously wants to have a foal of her own and I'll be pretty busy with Jacko for the rest of the year."

"Are you sure you want to turn her loose on the moor?" Sharon asked.

"Yes, why not? I promised her I would. I'm sure if she had the choice she'd rather be running wild on open moorland, living with all her friends and having babies. You see, Trifle spent the first six months of her life up here, so it'll be like coming home for her. She'll know most of the herd already – apart from the stallion, Peter Pan, of course. Our last stallion, Rifle, was Trifle's dad, but he's now with another herd."

"Oh, I get it! Rifle with a T in front makes Trifle!"

Sharon said. "Er, I don't doubt she wants a foal, but couldn't you bring the stallion in for a while, so she doesn't have to be turned away on the Common?"

"No! Don't you see? The whole point is I'm going to set her free!" Katy exclaimed.

"For your sake, or for hers?"

"For hers, of course!" Katy shouted.

"Okay, okay – she's your pony," Sharon replied calmly.

Katy rode on, trying to hide her disappointment. She'd been expecting Sharon to have the same reaction as Alice, saying nice things like, "Trifle's a very lucky pony, to have an owner like you." Instead, she'd sowed an annoying seed of doubt in Katy's mind.

As usual, the Exmoor Pony Society Stallion Parade and Annual General Meeting was held on the first Wednesday in May. But this year was special: Granfer was going to receive a presentation for his outstanding service to the Society after the AGM, so Katy was allowed the day off school to accompany him.

"What happens at the Stallion Parade, Granfer?" Katy asked as they drove across Exmoor.

"Well, I suppose the main point is that all the stallions which are available for breeding can be shown to any interested Exmoor pony owners, and it's also a chance for young stallions to be inspected for a license to breed. Good quality stallions whose owners are willing to receive other mares for breeding are awarded a premium."

"What's a premium?"

"Money."

"Why didn't we bring Peter Pan, then? We could have made some money!"

Granfer chuckled. "If you fancy catching him, taking him away from his mares, loading him into a horsebox and then leading him round a show ring with other stallions – when he hasn't been handled since he was a yearling – you're welcome to, my girl! Mind you, in the old days that's exactly what people did. Then, most of the stallions were unhandled and living with their herds on the moor. There were some fun and games at the Stallion Parade in those days, and no mistake! It was more like a rodeo than a parade, with several strong men hanging on to each stallion. Nowadays, most of the stallions are well-handled show ponies kept in fields and stables. Yes, it's certainly a very tame affair now, by comparison. Still, it's useful to see what's about. We'll be looking for a new stallion to run with the mares next year, and I happen to know that Mrs Soames is taking a very nice two-year-old colt to be inspected for a license today."

It wasn't a good idea to let closely related animals

breed with each other, so Granfer always changed his herd stallion every three years. Mrs Soames was an old friend who bred Exmoors on a farm near Withypool. She was a straightforward, no nonsense woman with a heart of gold and an encyclopaedic knowledge of Exmoor ponies. Katy thought she was wonderful.

"Oh, good. I'd like to see Mrs Soames again," Katy said.

Katy had a lovely morning, surrounded by Exmoor ponies and friendly people. Everyone talked non-stop about ponies, especially their own.

After a delicious roast dinner with a choice of three different puddings – Katy chose trifle, of course – it was time for the AGM. Granfer and other members of the committee sat at a long table facing everyone else sitting on chairs. Katy sat at the end of a row, with Mrs Soames next to her, and studied the agenda she'd been handed. This is going to take forever, she thought. She was right. Even the minutes of the last meeting seemed to drag on for ages. Her mind began to wander . . . Would she be able to get her geography homework done in time? What would the jumps be like at the indoor showjumping event next weekend? Should she send Greg a message on Facebook, or leave it a while? How was she going to ask Granfer about setting Trifle free? Would Trifle's foal be a filly or a colt? She thought too much about that and gave herself butterflies, so instead she started wondering what was for supper, even though she'd just eaten a large lunch.

After what seemed like an eternity, the AGM was over and the presentation was being made to Granfer. Katy was astonished by how many prizes he'd won over the years and how much work he'd done promoting Exmoor ponies. He was given a beautiful model of an Exmoor mare and foal. Trifle and foal, Katy thought fleetingly.

Granfer made a short speech of thanks before saying, "I'm so glad that my granddaughter, Katy, is with me today."

Everyone clapped. Some people swivelled round in their chairs to look at Katy. She felt her cheeks colouring.

"You see," Granfer continued, "this is an important day for me, not only because of your incredibly generous gift and good wishes but also because I've made a decision which involves all of you."

What on earth is Granfer going to say now? Katy wondered. With his audience on tenterhooks, he paused, took a sip of water from the glass in front of him and then smiled directly at her.

"I'd like you all to know that I'm giving my Exmoor ponies to Katy. They'll be hers from now on. I know that in her capable hands, the future of the Barton herd will be assured and the longstanding relationship between the Squires family and the Exmoor Pony Society will continue."

This time everyone stood up before they turned, clapping enthusiastically and smiling at Katy. She struggled to her feet, unsure whether her wobbly legs would hold her and certain that her cheeks were bright red. It was impossible to take in. The herd, *the whole herd*, was hers. Granfer had given her the Barton herd of Exmoor ponies!

A s they were driving home, an awful thought occurred to Katy. "Granfer?"

"Yup?"

"Um, you're not ill or anything, are you? I mean, that isn't why you've given me the herd is it?"

Granfer smiled and patted her knee affectionately. "Don't worry, I'm not planning on going for a good few years yet, but you never know what's around the corner, do you? My accident last year made me realise that. No, I just thought it would be far better for me to hand the herd over to you now, while I'm around to help you, than a few years down the line when I'll be of no use to anyone, most likely."

"Oh, I see. Thank goodness for that," Katy said. "I still can't believe you've given me the whole herd, you know. I used to long for just one pony, then I thought I was the luckiest person in the world because I had two, and now I've got . . . how many?"

"Let's see. The last time I checked there were forty-nine, but there are a few more foals to be born yet, so with Jacko and Trifle that makes fifty-one plus. Counting unborn foals, I expect you'll end up with around fifty-six ponies by mid-summer."

"Wow! Um, Granfer?"

"Yup?"

"Would . . . would it be okay if I let Trifle run with the herd this summer, so she can get in foal to Peter Pan?"

Granfer glanced at her, and grinned. "Up to you, my girl," he said. "After all, it's your herd now!"

9

Wild and Free

Katy decided to set Trifle free during half term at the end of May, so Alice would be there. Also, if Trifle did have a foal the following year it would be born from the end of April onwards – the best time of year, because in the summer the weather was warmer and food more plentiful.

Granfer, Rachel and Sharon also came over to witness the historic moment, and the guests who were staying at Barton Farm for a painting weekend were keen to join in, so quite a crowd made their way up to the Common gate.

Katy couldn't really believe that at long last the moment she'd been planning for ages had arrived. Tom rode the quad bike out over the Common to find the ponies and bring them back. Katy led Trifle through the gate, and waited.

"It's *so* romantic!" said a lady from the painting course. "I think you're wonderful to set your pony free from the shackles of domesticity, Katy!"

At that moment, the herd came charging over the horizon; a thundering mass of hooves and bodies moving as one. Trifle's head shot up, her nostrils flared and she began to quiver with excitement.

"Let her go, Katy!" Granfer urged. "Quickly now, before the ponies get too near."

With shaking hands, Katy fumbled with the buckle of the head collar. Trifle was tossing her head and dancing around, which didn't make the task any easier. At last, the buckle was undone and Trifle broke free. With her head held high and her tail raised like a flag, she galloped towards the ponies. The herd swerved, like a shoal of fish, and re-grouped behind Trifle, chasing her away over the Common and out of sight.

Katy felt totally empty. Everything had happened so quickly.

"Ah! Bless them! Wasn't it lovely how they all went off to play together?" said the lady from the painting course.

Katy knew enough about ponies to see they weren't really playing; they were ganging up against Trifle and chasing her. They no longer recognised her as one of their own, and they were travelling so fast that their herd instinct had taken over. Katy looked at Granfer, Rachel and Sharon, hoping for reassurance. She saw three worried faces.

Granfer caught her eye and forced a smile. "They should settle down after they've had a run around. Home for a cup of tea, I think."

"Sounds good to me!" the painting course lady declared happily.

Katy desperately wanted to run after the ponies and catch Trifle again – protect her from the hostile herd – but she knew it would be futile to try. Why had she been so stupid? Why hadn't she listened to Sharon? Why hadn't she thought this through?

They were all walking back across Moor Field when there was a dull thud of hooves behind them. They turned to see Trifle soaring over the Common gate. There were no other ponies in sight.

"Wow! I thought you said she couldn't jump!" Alice exclaimed.

Trifle galloped past at top speed and jumped another gate, heading for home as fast as her legs could carry her.

Katy found Trifle standing in her stable. Her sides

were heaving and her body was covered in frothy white sweat. In the adjoining stable, Jacko munched on some hay and seemed totally unconcerned. Katy stroked her pony's dripping neck. "I'm sorry. I'm so, so sorry," she murmured.

"Lucky the stable door was open, or she would have jumped that too!" Alice said, standing in the open doorway.

Sharon was behind her. "Is she okay?"

"I think so, apart from being puffed out. No wounds or anything obvious, anyway," said Katy. "I should have listened to you, Sharon. How did you know this wouldn't be a good idea?"

"I didn't know for certain, but I was just trying to see things from Trifle's point of view, that's all. It's plain she wants to be a mum – anyone can see that – but the herd isn't her family any more. You and Jacko are her family and the farm's her home. This is where she wants to be – she's just shown you that, loud and clear. Sensible pony, in my opinion. Freedom's very overrated; give me food, shelter and security any day."

Katy sighed. She was deeply touched that her pony had chosen to come home, but part of her felt sad that her dreams of Trifle running free on the moor and having a foal next spring wouldn't be realised.

*

The second half of the summer term went surprisingly quickly. Soon it was the summer holidays again, with Pony Club camp, competitions and shows. Katy and Jacko were promoted to class three with Anne Ruddock, and Katy won the prize for the most improved rider at camp. She and Jacko won a lot of rosettes in Pony Club competitions too. In many ways it was a golden time, as it was turning out to be one of the hottest, driest summers on record. The bed and breakfast guests at Barton Farm were delighted; they were getting a sun-drenched holiday without the hassle and expense of going abroad. The animals in the fields were not so happy; they melted into the shade of the beech hedges, trying to get away from the searing heat and an unrelenting plague of flies. Exmoor sizzled and shrivelled under the glare of the sun.

One day, towards the end of the summer holidays, Katy, Sharon and Alice went for a ride on the Common. Katy was on Trifle, Sharon was on Jacko and Alice was riding a lively young Arab mare called Sirocco, who'd been sent to Stonyford in the hope that lots of work would calm her down. Trifle and Jacko walked steadily while Sirocco side-stepped, jogged and cantered on the spot. In between coping with her pony's antics, Alice was telling her friends all about

Dean and Melanie's engagement, which had caused a lot of excitement in the neighbourhood. Alice and the twins were delighted and so, of course, was Melanie.

"I haven't seen her so happy for years! She's such fun again," Alice said. "And Dean's so lovely. He's really kind and very funny – not at all the brash city slicker we thought he was to begin with."

"Yes, I got that wrong, didn't I?" Katy admitted.

"I think *'You shouldn't judge people by appearances'* should become our motto, shouldn't it?" Sharon said.

The girls laughed, which upset Sirocco. Alice sat calmly while she exploded into the air with all four feet off the ground. "Dean's becoming an excellent rider, too. You never would have thought it possible would you?" she said.

Katy caught Sharon's eye, and they smiled at each other, remembering their ride on the Common in March, when they'd met Dean and Melanie.

They were riding down a pretty valley with a small stream running through it, surrounded by heather-clad slopes dotted with gorse bushes and hawthorn trees. The moorland was tinged with purple because the heather was just coming into flower. The air was heavy with scent. Insects hummed between the plants.

"Isn't it the most perfect day?" Katy said. "We haven't seen any ponies, though, have we? I wonder where they are."

"Right up on the top of the hill, I expect. Making the most of any breezes which'll keep the flies away." Sharon said.

"Were you a pony in another life? You always seem to know what they'll be thinking."

Sharon smiled. "No, but when you live with horses and ponies as much as I do, you soon get to know what makes them tick."

Katy smiled but she was only half-listening. There was something that didn't quite feel right. She sniffed the air. "Can you smell smoke?"

"Yes," Alice said. "Now you come to mention it, I can."

Sharon pointed at the hill behind them. "Oh, look! It *is* smoke!"

They turned their ponies, and saw grey smoke rising up into the blue sky.

"Someone must have decided to do some swaling," said Katy.

"What's swaling?" Sharon asked.

"Burning the old heather and dead grass to make way for new growth and control the ticks and things," Katy said, proud of her knowledge. She was determined to become a National Park ranger eventually. "It's a traditional way of managing the moor. People are allowed to do it, if they get permission first."

"Not in the summer, though!" Alice corrected her.

"It harms ground-nesting birds and other wildlife, and the peat can catch fire if it's dry – like it is now – which can be really bad for the environment. You see, peat stores greenhouse gases . . ."

"Honestly, Alice! You're such a know-it-all sometimes!" Katy interrupted, and regretted it instantly because Alice looked rather hurt. "I'm sorry," she added quickly. "I meant that as a joke."

"Well, the smoke doesn't look like a joke, anyway," said Sharon. "It looks pretty serious, to me. Let's get out of this valley so we can see what's going on."

They galloped up the steep hill out of the valley, with Sirocco flying ahead. When they reached the top they were aghast at what they saw. Irregular, fiery waves were creeping up the ridge of the Common, consuming the colourful moorland and leaving a blackened, smouldering wasteland on the lower slopes behind them.

Katy took her mobile phone from her pocket, and turned it on. "No signal," she said. There'll be a signal nearer to home, though. Let's go!"

"Hang on a minute!" said Alice. "What are those dark dots up on the ridge?"

"Oh, they must be the ponies!" cried Katy. "They'll get trapped by the fence at the top of the ridge if the fire keeps going. Come on, we must save them!"

"Wait a sec," said Alice. "I think I'd be more useful

raising the alarm. Sirocco won't be steady enough to cope with fire and a galloping herd, but she's really fast across country. I'll go back towards Barton Farm and I'll phone the fire brigade as soon as I get enough signal, okay?"

"Great idea," said Katy.

Alice set off at a flat-out gallop. "Good luck, both of you!" she yelled over her shoulder.

Katy and Sharon cantered steadily towards the fire. As they drew closer, they found that what they thought was one fire was, in fact, two. Although the wind was blowing the lines of flames towards each other, there was still an area which had escaped the fire in between. This, the girls decided, was the only route by which they could reach the Exmoor ponies and guide them to safety.

Trifle and Jacko were reluctant to go any closer, and the girls had to urge them on. In places, the smoke made it hard to pick a sensible passage through the heather and bracken. Several times, they had to re-trace their steps and change course. Fear gripped Katy. It felt like electric shocks running through her body and grabbing at her heart.

Eventually they reached the top of the ridge. The smoke thinned out, and they stood for a minute, trying to get some fresh air into their lungs and work out what to do next. It was clear that their plan to drive the Exmoor ponies down the hill through the smoke wasn't going to work. The ponies were in a panic. The fire and smoke had forced them onto the highest part of the Common, and they could go no further because of a boundary fence which ran along the top of the ridge. They were galloping to and fro along the fence line, looking for a way out. In their efforts to flee from the fire, they'd split into two groups and some mares had become separated from their foals, which added to the confusion. The shrill whinnies of the foals were heart-rending.

All the time, the flames were travelling towards them like a marching army. The boggy ground at the top of the ridge was so dry that it checked the fire only slightly, producing thick grey clouds of acrid smoke. There was only one way they could escape now, and that was over the fence.

"What shall we do? Drive them at it and hope they jump?" Katy yelled.

"No, they'll never jump that. We'll have to make it easier. It looks a bit more inviting over there!" Sharon shouted.

None of it looks inviting to me, Katy thought. She could see what Sharon meant, though. If they had to jump it, that would be a good place to try because the ground was on a gentle uphill slope. The fence consisted of sheep netting with two strands of barbed wire on top. The girls weren't wearing gloves or coats, so they had no means of protecting themselves from the sharp, vicious barbs in the wire.

Trifle was itchy and covered with sweat. She pawed at the ground and then bent her front legs, preparing to roll.

"Hup! Hup! You'll ruin your saddle!" Katy cried in dismay.

"That's the answer!" Sharon exclaimed. "Quick! If we take our numnahs from under our saddles, we can use them to protect us from the barbed wire." She dismounted, removed Jacko's saddle, took the numnah off and put it over the fence.

Katy did the same. As soon as her saddle had been removed, Trifle gave a deep sigh of satisfaction and rolled.

While Katy held the ponies, Sharon leaned on the numnahs and rocked vigorously from side to side, trying to break the wire. The wire sagged a little, but wouldn't break. Suddenly, with a splintering crack, a fence post snapped in two and the section of fence sank to half its original height.

"Hurray!" Katy shouted.

"That'll have to do, the fire's getting too close!" Sharon cried. "Get the saddles back on!"

Sharon was mounted on Jacko in no time, but Katy wrestled to get her girth done up. Either Trifle's getting expert at blowing her tummy out when I do up the girth or she's getting fatter, she thought. At last the saddle was secure, and Katy mounted.

"You go to the right, I'll go to the left and we'll try to herd all the ponies back to this bit of fence," Sharon said.

They went in a sweeping arc around the ponies, pushing them gently along the fence towards the broken section. The terrain was uneven; Katy had to hang on tight as Trifle dodged tussocks and leapt boggy patches.

The two groups were reunited, and the girls tried to drive the whole herd towards the jump they'd made. To their dismay, the ponies refused to go anywhere near the unfamiliar obstacle. The sound of the fire was getting louder by the minute; it was becoming hard to breathe the bitter, smoky air; heat radiated from the flames.

"I'll jump it first, to give the ponies a lead. You can push them on from behind. Try to keep them together. If it gets too dangerous, just get out," Sharon croaked, coughing between each word.

Katy gave her a thumbs up sign.

With Jacko leading them and Trifle pushing them on, the Exmoor ponies leapt over the makeshift jump and galloped away over the adjoining moorland. Then it was Trifle's turn to jump, and not a minute too soon;

the flames were roaring towards them. Fuelled by fear, they cleared the fence with ease and galloped over to where Jacko was standing. Within seconds, the fence posts were alight and wire was snapping in the heat. The numnahs caught fire, curled up and fell to the ground. Despite the heat, Katy shuddered, imagining how things could have turned out.

They heard the rumble of engines above the noise of the fire, and a four-wheel-drive fire truck appeared over the moor behind them, followed by Tom and Alice on a quad bike.

After making sure nobody was hurt, the firemen turned their attention to getting the blaze under control.

Tom hugged Katy. "You took your time!" she said cheekily.

"Your fault for finding a fire that's so difficult to reach! We had to go right round by the top road. We'll go away again, if you're going to be so ungrateful," Tom said, smiling.

"Not so fast, mister!" Katy said. "We've got to go and find my Exmoor ponies!"

They found the ponies in the next valley, drinking from a cool stream.

"Are they all there?" Katy asked anxiously.

"Fifty-five, counting the foals as well," Tom said.

Katy was always amazed by his ability to count

livestock quickly. "Fifty-five wild ones and two tame ones makes fifty-seven. They're all here!" she exclaimed, hugging Sharon, Jacko, Alice, Tom and Trifle in turn. "We did it!" she exclaimed. "We saved every one of them!"

10

Tinkerbell

"That Exmoor of yours is as big as a bus. What on earth are you feeding her?" Granfer asked as he looked over the stable door.

"Only silage, Granfer. Honest!" Katy said, stroking Trifle's neck as she ate some food in a bucket. "Oh, and just a handful of nuts when she comes in at night. Jacko gets a good feed every night because he's fit and clipped out for all the competitions we're doing this winter. I don't want Trifle to feel left out, just because I'm not riding her very much."

"Well, you can easily kill ponies with kindness, you

know," Granfer said. "If you give her too much food she'll get laminitis, which will make her feet so painful that she'll go hopping lame. Yes, laminitis is a terrible disease; some ponies never recover from it."

"I know, Granfer. We're taught about all that sort of thing at Pony Club. I must admit, she does seem to be getting pretty fat, doesn't she? But she's not at all lame. It's probably just her thick winter coat making her look big. I'll try to ride her a bit more, now it's the Christmas holidays."

"Good idea," Granfer said.

The following day, Katy discovered that Trifle really had become fatter. When she put the saddle on, the girth was too short by several inches. She decided to ride Trifle bareback to Wellsworthy, as a gentle start to her fitness programme.

As Katy had feared, something did seem to be wrong. Trifle was much more sluggish than usual, although she didn't feel lame. She urged Trifle into a trot, but soon let her walk again because she was breathing so heavily. Perhaps Granfer was right; she'd made Trifle ill from over-feeding her. His harsh words about killing ponies with kindness kept ringing in her ears, and she only noticed an unfamiliar Land Rover parked outside Wellsworthy when she was almost next to it.

A moment later, a man came out of the front door. He was tall, sandy-haired and deeply suntanned. Katy's heart flipped. "Greg!"

"G'day, Katy!" he said, smiling his special smile as he walked towards her.

She felt flustered. "What on earth are you doing here?"

"That's a nice way to greet your new neighbour."

Katy blushed. This was the moment she'd been dreaming about for months, and she was ruining it. "Wow! You're *living* here?"

"That's right. Dean's over at Stonyford now, but he doesn't want to sell Wellsworthy so I'm renting it from him. I was going to settle in Australia, but then this came up so I've decided to grab the opportunity. I hope you don't mind." Greg put his hand on Trifle's mane. His eyes met Katy's, making her heart flip again.

"Mind! Why should I mind? I think it's brilliant!" she exclaimed. Then, embarrassed by her own enthusiasm, she added, "You see, Dad and Tom were worried Wellsworthy might be converted into holiday lets or something."

"Well, I won't do holiday lets, but I am planning to start another business here."

"Oh?"

Greg smiled. "Yes, bottled water."

"But there's water everywhere you look on Exmoor, and it's free!" Katy said.

"Exactly. That's why it's such a good plan."

"What gave you the idea?" Katy asked.

"You did."

"*Me?*"

"Yes. You sent me that bottle of water in Australia. It made me realise how much we take water for granted on Exmoor, and what a valuable commodity it is when it's scarce, as it was in Australia. I started to think that, if I were ever lucky enough to get somewhere to live on Exmoor, I'd set up a business bottling water. When Dean offered me Wellsworthy, it was too good to be true. Wellsworthy's always been famous for its plentiful supply of natural spring water – hence the name."

"Is Dean okay about it all?"

"He thinks it's a great idea, The farm only has sixty-five acres with it, so I'll have to do something besides farming to make ends meet. Selling water seems to be the answer. There's a growing market for mineral water, even in this country. In fact – believe it or not – it's often more expensive than milk. But, unlike milk, it has a very long shelf life. So, have I managed to persuade you I'm not off my rocker?"

Katy giggled. "Just about."

"Good, because I've got a job for you," Greg said. "Will you design a label for me?"

"What sort of label?"

"A label for my bottled water. An Exmoor scene with Wellsworthy Water above it would be good."

Katy was amazed. "Why me?"

"Because I love your drawings and paintings, especially that painting of moorland you did for your dad – the one that's hanging in your the kitchen."

Greg loves my paintings! Katy thought happily. "Of course I'll do some drawings. I'll do several, then you can choose," she said.

"Proper job. I'll drop in to see your family later, if that's okay."

"We'll look forward to it," Katy replied. "I'll tell Dad to get the whisky bottle out." He was famous for the generous measures of whisky he gave to visitors.

"At least I'll be able to walk home from Barton, now I'm living here at Wellsworthy!"

Katy laughed. "You need to get a horse to take you home." She roused Trifle, who seemed to have gone to sleep on her feet while they'd been talking. "See you later, then. Promise you'll come?"

"Of course. I'll look forward to it."

Trifle seemed to be a bit more eager on the way home, and Katy's earlier concerns about her pony melted away because of her excitement over their new neighbour. She couldn't wait to tell her family the good news.

*

When Katy fed Trifle and Jacko their pony nuts that evening, Trifle wasn't interested in hers. She'd never been off her food before. Katy started to worry again, and she went out to check her several times that evening. Deep down, Katy could sense there was something wrong, but whatever it was didn't seem to get any better or worse until she looked in on her ponies before going to bed.

Trifle appeared to be rather uncomfortable and restless, and she hadn't eaten much hay. Perhaps she's getting colic, Katy thought. They'd been taught about colic at Pony Club, so she knew how serious it could be. Should she call Granfer or Rachel to ask their advice? She looked at her watch. It was eleven-thirty – they'd probably be asleep. What could she do? It was too cold to stay in the stable all night. She'd just have to go to bed, get a bit of sleep and come out again in another couple of hours.

She couldn't sleep. At two o'clock she went outside again. The frosty night air sliced into her lungs and chilled her through. Trifle looked much the same, but Katy could see from her straw bedding that she'd been very restless. She stood watching until her kneecaps started jumping up and down and she couldn't stand the cold any longer. "I'll just go in and get a hot water bottle and a sleeping bag, and then I'll come and stay with you for the rest of the night, okay?" Katy said.

Inside the farmhouse once more, she made herself some hot chocolate, drank it at the kitchen table, filled a hot water bottle with the rest of the water in the kettle and took it upstairs to her bedroom. There, she fished out her sleeping bag from a cupboard and put on some more clothes. She sat on her bed to put on an extra pair of socks, and it felt so comfy that she lay back on the pillows for a second, hugging her hot water bottle.

Katy woke with a start. Her watch said five-fifteen. Oh, no! Trifle! She jumped off her bed, rushed downstairs, pulled on her boots and ran to the stable. How could she have slept for that long? If Trifle were dead it would all be her fault!

With her heart in her mouth, she turned on the stable light. Jacko had been sleeping standing up. He woke with a start. She could hardly bear to look in the other stable for fear of what she might find.

At least Trifle was still alive! But her bedding was really churned up and she appeared to be eating the straw in the corner of her box, which was odd because she still had plenty of hay left. With alarm, Katy also noticed that her neck and flanks were sweaty – another sign of colic. Time to call the vet, I think, Katy said to herself. Trifle lifted her head, then looked back at the straw in the corner, and made a tender, whuffling sort of noise.

Katy peered into the darkness. For a moment her mind couldn't believe what her eyes were telling her. There, nestled in the far corner of the stable, was a perfect, wonderful, adorable, magical, tiny foal!

Carefully, Katy entered the stable and approached the corner, keeping an eye on Trifle to make sure she didn't mind. The foal was very new; steam rose from its shivering body into the cold early morning air. Katy rubbed the little creature with straw to dry it and get its circulation going. Soon it tried to struggle to its feet in short, uncoordinated bursts of energy. With Katy's help it stood for the first time, spindly legs braced and shaking with the effort. Gently she manoeuvred the foal so it was standing in the right position to drink some life-giving first milk from the udder between Trifle's hind legs. All the while, Katy talked in a soothing voice: "There's a good girl. What a clever pony you are. What a clever girl. There we are. Shall we try a drink, then? Clever old girl." Am I dreaming? She wondered. Is this really happening? It felt as if her whole body would burst with the amount of love which had flooded into her.

The foal suckled greedily from its mother, and then crumpled onto the straw again. Katy sat down with her back against the stable wall, and stroked its unusually thick, downy hair as it slept. Nature must have given it a fluffy winter coat, Katy thought. Nature's pretty

wonderful. In fact, everything's pretty wonderful . . .
She drifted off to sleep.

An hour later, Tom found Katy asleep in Trifle's
stable, her arms draped over a dozing newborn foal.
Trifle was lying down close by.

News of the foal spread rapidly. Before long Mum,
Dad, Tom, Alice, Melanie, Dean, Granfer, Greg,
Sharon and Rachel were all crowded into Trifle's stable
as the good-natured pony munched on some hay.

"What are you going to call it? Is it a he or a she?"
Alice asked.

"I've been so excited, I haven't even looked!" Katy
said. She examined the foal quickly. "It's a she!" she
announced.

"So, what are you going to call her, then?" Alice
asked.

"I've absolutely no idea."

"That's rather a long name!" Alice teased. "And the
championship goes to Katy Squires on I've Absolutely
No Idea!" she said, pretending to talk through a
loudspeaker.

Alice and Katy spent the rest of the morning thinking
about possible names for the foal, but nothing seemed
to fit.

*

After lunch, Katy's mum asked the girls to decorate the Christmas tree. The old familiar boxes of decorations were carried down from the attic and placed by the side of the tree. Half-forgotten memories came with them, from pine cones covered with glitter which Katy had made at primary school to a nativity scene which Gran and Granfer had bought just after Dad was born. The girls unpacked the decorations carefully so they could plan where everything would go. They were aware of the great responsibility which had been given to them.

"Tinsel!" Alice said triumphantly, lifting some silver tinsel out of a box.

"What?"

"Call the foal Tinsel. It's Christmassy and it keeps the Barton herd tradition of the foal's name starting with the first letter of the dam's name. I think she looks like a Tinsel, don't you?"

Katy secretly wondered how an Exmoor pony could look like a Tinsel.

"Perhaps," she said doubtfully, not wanting to hurt Alice's feelings. "But *ideally* it should tie in with the stallion's name as well."

"You don't want much, do you?" Alice replied. "Okay. Peter Pan . . . Who are the characters in the book? I can only think of Nana and Wendy, and they don't begin with T . . . Oh, look! Here's the fairy for the top of the tree."

"That's it! You're a genius, Alice!"

"What?"

"The foal's name, of course! Something to do with Christmas and the story of Peter Pan, and beginning with T! Tinkerbell! She was the fairy in Peter Pan, wasn't she? Eureka! We've done it! Tinkerbell!" Katy exclaimed. "Why didn't we think of it before? It's perfect! Oh, I must go and tell Granfer." She headed for the door, but then stopped. "On second thoughts, let's make an announcement at tea."

Christmas Eve tea at Barton Farm had become a traditional feast. All Katy's family were there: Dad, Mum, Tom, Granfer, Gran, Rachel, Mark and Heather. Several friends had also been invited: Melanie, Dean, Alice, the twins, Sharon and Greg.

When everyone was seated, Katy said, "I have an announcement to make! Alice and I have come up with a name for the foal. Her mum's Trifle and her dad's Peter Pan, so we thought Tinkerbell would be a good name."

There was a general flurry of conversation about how appropriate it was, and then Granfer said, "You're sure Peter Pan's the father, then?"

Katy stared at him. "Yes, of course. I mean, who else could it be?"

"Any one of several stallions hereabouts," Granfer said matter-of-factly. "May not even have been an Exmoor stallion. Think about it. She must have got into foal late January or early February. Well, unless you know something we don't, she was back here at the farm and Peter Pan was away out on the Common then, so how could they have got together?"

Katy felt on the verge of tears. She *knew* Peter Pan was Tinkerbell's father. He had to be!

Tom stood up and cleared his throat. "Er, I was hoping I'd be able to keep this a secret but, as Granfer says, the truth always comes out in the end. You see, Mum and Dad, when you were away in London there was a terrific storm one night and several gates were damaged, including the Common gate. The whole herd broke into Moor Field and tucked into those silage bales which should have been fenced off. Mark had to come and re-wrap the bales, and then I fenced them off immediately afterwards. As Granfer also says, a lazy man always makes work for himself!"

There was a rumble of amusement.

"But I'm afraid that's not all," Tom continued. "On the same night, Jacko and Trifle broke out of their field and somehow joined the herd in Moor Field; I found them all together the next morning. It was a hard job to separate them out again, too, I can tell you. Anyway, the long and the short of it is that Peter Pan was with

Trifle for several hours and I think that's proof beyond reasonable doubt that he's the father, don't you?"

Katy got up from her chair, ran round the table and hugged her brother. "I knew it wasn't rats!" she whispered in his ear. "Thanks, Tom!"

They ate, drank, talked and played games until the evening turned into the night.

"Dad always says that the farm animals talk at midnight on Christmas Eve, don't you, Dad?" Katy's dad said as he dealt some cards.

Dean laughed. "Nothing would surprise me in this magical place! What do they say, Jack?"

"Ah, that's something you'll have to find out for yourself," Granfer replied.

It was nearly midnight when the guests left. Katy went outside to check her ponies. They were all fine.

"Goodnight, Trifle, my wonderful, clever pony!" she said. "Goodnight, little Tinkerbell. Goodnight, Jacko, my handsome boy. Happy Christmas!"

As Katy turned to go, she was sure she heard Trifle say, "Happy night!"

Well, it was Christmas Eve, so anything was possible.

What a lot can happen in one year, Katy thought when she woke up on Christmas morning.

Jacko was fit and well again, Heather had been born, Granfer had given Katy the Exmoor ponies, they'd escaped that terrible fire, Melanie and Dean were going to get married, Alice was still her best friend but Sharon had become a good friend too, Greg was living at Wellsworthy and Trifle had given birth to Tinkerbell. Things just couldn't get any better than that, could they?

Katy sighed with happiness and stretched out in her warm bed. Her feet bumped against something. It was a bulging Christmas stocking, waiting to be explored.

Author's Note

Authors are often asked where their ideas come from. Well, my ideas are often inspired by my own experiences. For instance, I live on an Exmoor hill farm with sheep, cattle and Exmoor ponies, and we have a free-living herd of Exmoor ponies on an area of moorland above the farm. One stormy night, our ponies broke through the gate between the moorland and a field where all the silage bales were stacked. My husband Chris had been meaning to fence off the bales, but had never got around to it. The ponies made a terrible mess, and we had to re-wrap a lot of the silage in the middle of winter. Having read this story, does that sound familiar?

All the human and equine characters in this series are fictional, but many people and ponies I've known throughout my life have given me inspiration in one way or another. For example, Katy was the name of my best friend at my first school, and a wonderful neighbouring farmer who was a great countryman was called Granfer by his family.

Of the ponies which have helped me with this book, a Welsh cob called Jacko and an Exmoor pony called Tinkerbell have been particularly important.

Jacko was my first pony, and to me he was the best pony in the world. Like the Jacko in this story, he was a handsome liver chestnut gelding who was safe, reliable and fun. His only fault was that he had soft hooves. Sometimes he lost a shoe in the field, and once he trod on the upturned nails and went hopping lame.

Tinkerbell is slow and arthritic now, but she used to be a bundle of energy. She was our daughter Sarah's pony when they were both much younger. Both she and Sarah gave me lots of ideas for these stories about Katy and Trifle. We were so fond of Tinkerbell that we didn't want to sell her after Sarah had grown out of her. As Tinks is a mare, we thought it would be a great idea to let her run free with the ponies on the moor so she could lead a natural lifestyle and have some foals of her own. However, within minutes of being set loose she'd galloped back to our farm, jumping all the obstacles in her way. We found her standing in her stable, covered in sweat. She'd told us where she wanted to live, and we never tried to set her free again. Later that year, and for two subsequent years, we brought the stallion to her in the hopes that she'd get in foal but – unlike Trifle in this story – she never did. Instead she's earned her keep as a good friend to any horse or pony in need of some company.

Lots of things I've experienced in my life have made their way into *Katy's Pony Surprise*. Yes, I was the girl who forgot to check her girth before mounting on the first day of Pony Club camp *and* I spilt ketchup down my jods at a smart horse show. A more pleasant childhood memory is that my grandmother taught me how to decorate a Christmas tree.

Oh, and at midnight on Christmas Eve we always go down to the farm buildings, just in case the animals are talking . . .

It's hard to mention individual people who have helped me with this book for fear of leaving someone out, but friends who have given me particular help and encouragement are Marcia Monbleau, Sally Chapman-Walker, Sue Baker, Sue Croft and my mum.

Most of all, thanks and love to Chris, my very patient

and understanding husband, and our children, George and Sarah.

Last, but not least, many thanks to Fiona Kennedy, Felicity Johnston and the team at Orion for all their invaluable guidance and hard work.

This year I named one of our Exmoor foals Orion, because I was so delighted that Orion Children's Books wanted to publish my stories. Keep up to date with his progress on my website!

Victoria Eveleigh
North Devon
December 2011

Exmoor Ponies

Exmoor ponies, or 'Exmoors' as they are often called, are a very special breed. They are the only native pony breed that has the same characteristics as the original British Hill Pony that came to the British Isles about one hundred and thirty thousand years ago. Various studies of the bones, teeth and genetics of Exmoor ponies have supported this.

Why Exmoor ponies have survived as nature intended, whereas other breeds have been altered by man, is a bit of a mystery. Historically, Exmoor was a wild, sparsely populated area, which was reserved as a Royal Forest or hunting ground. There were no significant trade routes through the area, and no important towns nearby. It seems that, because of this, Exmoor had little contact with the rest of Britain and the wild ponies within the Forest remained an isolated, pure population.

In 1818, the Forest was sold to an industrialist called John Knight. Several local farmers bought some of the wild ponies and started up herds of their own, including the former warden of Exmoor Forest, Sir Thomas Acland. He founded the Acland herd, now the Anchor herd, which can be seen on Winsford Hill.

The Exmoor Pony Society was founded in 1921, with the purpose of keeping the breed true to type.

During the Second World War, many ponies were stolen for food and fewer ponies were bred. In the end, only about forty-six mares and four stallions were left on Exmoor. A remarkable lady called Mary Etherington encouraged some Exmoor farmers to re-establish their herds so that the breed was saved. However, it is still classified as endangered by the Rare Breeds Survival Trust.

Exmoor ponies make history come to life. It is up to all of us to ensure they have a future.

If you'd like to find out more about Exmoor ponies, the Exmoor Pony Society has a very good website www.exmoorponysociety.org.uk with lots of information and details of ponies for sale or loan. The secretary is called Sue McGeever, and her telephone number is (01884) 839930.

A visit to Exmoor isn't complete without a trip to the Exmoor Pony Centre, near Dulverton. This is the headquarters of the Moorland Mousie Trust, a charity dedicated to the welfare and promotion of Exmoor ponies. Admission to see the ponies and their pony-themed gift shop is free, but you can also book pony handling sessions for beginners or rides on the moor for experienced riders. For details see the website www.exmoorponycentre.org.uk or telephone (01398) 323093. The Trust runs a pony adoption scheme – the next best thing to owning an Exmoor pony!

Want the chance to adopt a pony

at the EXMOOR PONY CENTRE for one year?

Adopt an **EXMOOR PONY!**

ALL YOU HAVE TO DO TO ENTER IS EMAIL:

competitions@orionbooks.co.uk

with the subject heading "Exmoor Pony" and one lucky winner will win a year's pony sponsorship.